**PURE
SLUSH
BOOKS**

inane

Pure Slush Volume #14

First published as a collection May 2017

Pure Slush Books
4 Warburton Street
Magill SA 5072
Australia

Email: edpureslush@live.com.au
Website: http://pureslush.webs.com
Store: http://pureslush.webs.com/store.htm

Original front cover photo *Assorted Toys* by Pam Boyd
Cover design by Matt Potter

ISBN: 978-1-925536-17-1

Also available as an eBook
ISBN: 978-1-925536-18-8

A note on differences in punctuation and spelling

Pure Slush Books proudly features writers from all over the English-speaking
world. Some speak and write English as their first language, while for others,
it's their second or third or even fourth language. Naturally, across all versions
of English, there are differences in punctuation and spelling, and even in
meaning. These differences are reflected in the work *Pure Slush Books*
publishes, and it accounts for any differences in punctuation, spelling and
meaning found within these pages.

Contents

How Jacqueline Bouvier Changed the World

by

J P Lundstrom

She didn't do it by marrying a future president. It wasn't her marriage to an aging playboy shipping magnate, either. It was a small thing.

You see, girls used to wear only dresses. No jeans, no shorts. Little girls in colder climes may have worn snowsuits; I saw them in books. But in southern California, we never saw a snowflake, much less a snowsuit.

When girls went outside they wore play dresses. After a few months a dress just wasn't what it had been. The sleeves didn't stay puffy and the sashes drooped. So the year's school dresses were downgraded for play. In a play dress you could get dirty. You could even hang upside-down from a tree.

Our mothers wore dresses specially made for working around the house. They were not attractive, and they were not intended to be seen. If a woman left the house during the day to buy groceries, she changed clothes.

Where does Jacqueline Bouvier come into all this? Bear with me.

I suspect the change began when women went to work in the factories during WWII. I do know that right around the time General Eisenhower became President Eisenhower, we got a break.

Wearing pedal pushers, pants that came just below the knee, a girl could ride a bike and not get caught in the chain. A good idea, but not for school. Still, anything was better than climbing a tree in a play dress and having the neighborhood boys start chanting. It must be genetic, for even at that tender age, the males were fixated on what was beneath a girl's skirt.

After that, pedal pushers became Capris. Women started wearing pants in public, and it was not only acceptable, it was *fashionable.*

But not jeans yet, except for a few who adopted the James Dean look, with a white shirt and a little silk scarf tied around the neck. (If you don't believe me, watch an old movie.)

I wore a dress every day in high school. Or a skirt and sweater. Or a skirt and blouse, sometimes with a little silk scarf tied around the neck.

Here's the part about Jacqueline Bouvier.

One day I opened a magazine and saw Jacqueline Bouvier Kennedy Onassis, as they used to write. She strolled along some beachfront with her teenage daughter, wearing jeans and a white tee-shirt. And, as one could see, no bra. Of course, she had the figure for it.

Her fashion forwardness had a world-wide impact. Manufacturers cranked up their production facilities. Levis were copied from Paris, France to Paris, Texas.

And people were put to work creating inane slogans. I know you've seen them: *Damn, I'm good*, or *I'm with Stupid.*

How many women in dresses do you see today? Compare that to the number of women you see in jeans and a tee-shirt who *don't* have the figure for it.

You see what I mean? *That* is how Jacqueline Bouvier changed the world.

Looking Log 004: Dress Code

by
AJ Huffman

I broke down and went shopping. It usually
cheers me up, but what a nightmare. Here,
these people are all powder blue pinafores
and stalkings. (I didn't even know they still made
those things!) I look like I should change
my name to Heidi, take up yodeling
on a Swiss Mountain somewhere. I swear,

even the mirror laughed.

The Rockstar and The Turnip

by

Stephenson Muret

"I'm a big fan of the turnip, Sammy," the fan confessed to the rockstar. The fan had never met a rockstar before. He won his backstage pass in a radio station contest guessing the number of baby bottles necessary to drain a keg of Pabst. Now, for the first time in his life, he stood beside a real celebrity.

"The Turnips?" the rockstar replied politely. The guitar virtuoso peered into middle distance. "I don't think I've heard of them."

"No?" pursued the fan.

The rockstar shook his head tentatively, reflectively.

"Maybe you've never been in the garden in the fall," the fan offered. "You are more likely to see them there in the fall."

"In The Garden? You mean Madison Square?"

"Yeah. Whichever. Or in the market."

The rockstar gazed, thoughtful. He mouthed, "The Market?"

"I'm a really big fan. I love it in the fall when it's easy to find them. Sometimes I go to the market and buy ten or twenty. They're kinda like a cross between a carrot and a potato for me. I don't like to eat them raw that much. That's more a carrot thing for me. But, my, when you make them into a soup with some onion, a little sage, black pepper and nutmeg, and then add some evaporated milk and butter you got something really special, I'll tell you. Nothing like it. Sometimes I make gigantic pots of this and then freeze thirteen or fourteen bowls worth so I can have it anytime I want. Sometimes in the morning even. It's more a lunch thing for me ultimately. But I love it. I'm a really big fan of the turnip, Sammy."

The fan grinned eagerly. He did not customarily chatter so much, but here he stood, philosophizing with Sammy Toughguy, the famous Sammy Toughguy. He thought to quieten for a bit so Sammy could contribute too, but then he just couldn't stop himself.

"You know turnips are supposed to be good for the liver. And the leaves of the plant benefit the colon, scientists say. The scientific name for them is Brassica Rapa. There is also a Brassica Napus which is the yellow turnip which is also sometimes referred to as the rutabaga. Rutabagas do not have the same sweetness as your average Brassica Rapa. Especially in that soup. They are a little sharper. That's why I always make it clear to new acquaintances that I am a fan of the turnip, not the rutabaga. It's the turnip I'm a fan of, Sammy. Not the rutabaga."

The rockstar squinted at the fan. He heh-hehed.

"Lookit," said the fan. "If you were to boil a couple of turnips with an onion for an hour or so and add a little sage and nutmeg and evaporated milk and butter, you would never regret it. It's good for your liver. It might even clear up your complexion a little."

The fan nodded, definitively.

And the rockstar leaned slightly away, coughing toward his bodyguard. "Karlo," he hemmed. "Story time over. Get this guy off me."

Karlo Strongman then hovered beside the fan, to usher the fan away from Sammy Toughguy and toward the room's double doors. As the fan shuffled out, he insisted, perplexedly: "But it's true! I promise! The butter makes it divine!"

A Lesson About Priorities

by
Eliza Redwood

can i go 2 the bathroom?

No.

can I go to the bathroom?

No.

Can I go to the bathroom?

I don't know—

Can you go to the bathroom?

Fine. *May* I—

too late.

Pablo Neruda fails to seduce a lover

by
Allan J. Wills

To be sure, I looked it up in the dictionary: inane, after inamorato and before inanimate. Strange, how seemingly unrelated things can be arranged like that. For my lover it would be an empty boast, an inanity, to say to her "I love you." She is only alive to actions. True lovers hardly need words to know each other's hearts.

'I want to do with you what spring does with the cherry trees.' Maybe these words worked for Neruda because the elements preceding this final line of his poem are such an unrestrained and intimate exploration of an emotionally complex relationship. His poem is an expression of insight into, and gift to, his lover. "This is the nature of our love. All this precedes desire." The desire is made tangible only at the end. It is a complicated "I love you."

For most of us, poetry makes a poor love-language. To know my lover's mind I watch and listen, listening to her and sharing ideas, her ideas, rather than gossip about other people and things. Anticipating her moods, making breakfast for her, keeping the house tidy, taking the kids to the park to give her time alone, and smiling with pleasure on seeing her in the morning and after work, these are small gifts that make her blossom. Gifts of objects are not important to her. They are inanimate clutter.

So

by
Jeffrey Zable

I've written over two thousand poems and published at least a thousand yet my next door neighbor doesn't even know that I write. When we talk, it's mainly about how hard it's getting to find parking anywhere in the city, or she'll remind me that's it's garbage day on Friday if we should meet on a Thursday afternoon. Other than that I sometimes wonder if I'll get to a point in which I have nothing left to say in my writing, and like Hemingway I'll rig something up so I won't have to suffer the deep, deep depression. Actually I can't say that the writing of poems gives me much solace except during those times when what comes out amazes me, and I say to myself, "Hey, I must be one of the best poets of my generation, or at least one of the better ones!" Telling myself this shores me up, and I walk around thinking I'm really some hotshot for having such a way with words—like my poems mean more than what everyone else says or does in the world and somehow, some way, everyone will get hip to this if I just give them time.

Anvil D'amore

by
E. M. Stormo

When *Looney Tunes* was first shown to European audiences in the late '40s, the comedic use of anvils caused a mild "anvil hysteria", especially in parts of rural France, helping to break the family mold decades before the sexual decadency of the post-war era had fully set in, as some men were known to become infatuated with these "iron rhinos" at a young age.

Mrs. DuBois blamed "those American cartoons," while Mr. DuBois disagreed. He railed against "the village's high concentration of tall smoky men covered in black sweat."

To Oliver DuBois, all anvils were made of a single steel he loved, and "she" was always the same anvil no matter which blacksmith he visited.

On his twelfth birthday, Oliver proposed to "her" with a self-forged ring.

"*Oui*," she said, as he slid it onto her horn.

Mrs. DuBois caught him crafting verses of poetry around the English phrase "rhino baby", and hoped his infatuation had moved onto something at least living, though no less sinful, but Oliver had adopted this Americanism and other unnatural names in order to disguise his enduring passion.

When they were alone, she was his *anvil d'amore* once more. How he loved the way she fell from the sky onto the unsuspecting head.

Positive Feedback

by
Rob Walker

she said she liked north

of 80% of my

work

and i thanked her

assuming that north

is good

To Protect Against the Bites of Sharks

by
Gordon Brown

To protect against the bites of sharks, I have covered my horse in mousetraps. She's a good horse, and a reliable one, even if she looks more like a minivan than a knightly steed. Even if she eats gas instead of grass. Even if she's made out of metal and rubber and plastic and can seat a family of eight with ample room in the trunk and 35 MPGs on the highway. But she keeps the sharks away, there's no doubt of that. I haven't seen one for miles. You might say that this is because I live in the middle of the desert, but what's a desert if not an ocean without the excessive humidity?

To protect against the bites of sharks I have taken to disguise myself as one of their kind. This has proven difficult as shark costumes are in short supply, so I have had to settle for disguising myself as Dracula instead. I do, however, wear a pin on my lapel reading shark sympathizer, and this should be sufficient. I have also changed my e-mail to sharkfan1000, just to be certain.

To protect against the bites of sharks, I am sure never to answer my door. Once my ex-wife tried to get in, claiming she had forgotten her keys. I told her to come to the window so I could toss them down. Instead I hurled a special edition DVD boxset of the movie *Jaws*, the pointy end of which caught her on the temple. She shrieked at me and called me all manner of foul things, and for a moment I feared I had made a grievous error. But as she turned I could see the unmistakable lines of rigid gills and the lumps in her dress where it stretched over her dorsal fins.

Just so that you know I'm not crazy.

November Ninth

by
Flora Gaugg

I stood underneath the dappled shade of a tree (I like to get a little sun during my lunch break, but not too much) and watched him. Absent smile, dishevelled hair. Probably homeless. Probably mentally deficient in some way. People like him are a common sight in the city parklands. If I had stopped to think about his situation I'm sure I would have felt very sad for him (but I only had half an hour and I wanted to enjoy my chickpea salad).

He was throwing something into the branches of a tree. I couldn't see what it was. I watched it fly up, then back down. He picked it up and launched it into the tree again. His persistence was admirable, if not a little unnerving. I only realised the object was a dead bird when he began plucking feathers from its body and releasing them into the air (it probably would have put me off my lunch, had I not been quite so hungry). Again and again he hurled the naked little body into the tree. Mustn't judge, I told myself.

Meanwhile, in the United States of America, a new president was being elected.

We Walked Beneath a Streetlamp

by
Stephen V. Ramey

In the walk we took after our latest fight, I noticed a decorative street lamp fixed to the wall, its base precisely aligned with the division between paint and bare brick of adjoining buildings.

"You see that?" I said. "That's what I'm talking about."

"What about it?" Janet said. White flashed as her eyeballs turned up. I thought of the texture of her, the sinew and straw hair, lip balm on my kiss, liquor in her mouth. She read mysteries at night while I lay beside her, stewing over runny eggs in the morning, fuzzy slippers on her feet. Nothing about her was right these days.

"That's our marriage," I said.

She shrugged. "A light that's out? Sure, I guess."

"Not that," I said. "Why would a light be on in daytime? Use that brain once in a while, Janet. No, it's the housing, the arm, the bolts, everything."

"Rusted? Ready to crumble?"

"No!" I shouted, and the whole street stood still. "Paint protects it from rust, you imbecile."

"Call me that again," Janet said, "and you'll have divorce papers in your hand tomorrow."

Vigor leaked from me like a steam trail. "Sorry."

Janet nodded once. "Okay, I'm curious. How is our marriage like a street lamp, Arthur?"

"Not a street lamp. That particular one. You see how it stands out from the wall, the way the support tapers to a point where it connects to the lamp housing?"

"I guess so," Janet said.

"That's our marriage. Beyond solid grasp, slipping out of reach. We've forgotten to keep it close."

Janet huffed. "I haven't forgotten. It's just not worth the effort."

"How can you say that? We've been together a dozen years."

"Is that all?"

"Oh come on," I said. "There was a spark. It's not been that long since you wanted to make love to me."

Janet laughed. "Make love? It's such a curious expression. I think of a magician pulling a rabbit out of a hat, or maybe stuffing one in... repeatedly."

We came to an intersection. The traffic light was about to turn. I held out my arm to stop Janet.

"What is it you want?" I said. "Romance? I can do that. There's a flower shop a block from here."

"What I want," she said, "is something new. A little excitement."

The anger boiled up again. "Are you seeing someone else?"

Janet glanced back at the streetlamp. "Apparently not." She stepped down from the curb.

Meth'

by
Melisa Quigley

John walked out of the house in his underwear. His hands jittered and he lit a cigarette and drew back on it. The smoke curling reminded him of rubbing two sticks together to light a campfire in his boy scout days. A gust of wind swirled through his long hair and rain spat in his face. A trickle of blood ran down his arm from a fresh puncture wound at his elbow. His eyes held a vacant stare and he strode over the broken pavement and bumped a man coming out of McDonalds. He shoved the door open and hastened to the counter. The girl serving cringed when she saw him.

"I'm here for me meth'," said John.

"You've got the wrong store. The chemist is on the next corner," she said.

Talking in Threes

by
Jerry Vilhotti

"There are people in here who see fuken five hundred pound flies," Tom whispered in her ear. He nodded three times saying he knew he needed rest rest rest and sleep sleep sleep to forget their restaurant that was going bankrupt. He tried to rip a napkin in half to convince her that he understood, but could not, and in frustration began to hit himself in the head with a closed fist; imitating what his father did when angry.

"See? See? See? They're going to think I'm really crazy. I know I need rest, rest, rest," Tom said as he patted Rhoda's head gently to stop her sobbing while he smiled at all the sedated people walking about them.

Rhoda would sign him out that afternoon and he would be free once again to go find Christ but she would stop the journey with a lithium pill that would make him become the headshrinker that would make heads grow into all directions.

Tidying-Up

by
Jane Banning

"Let's clean out the woods!" she emails.

"Let's not," I reply.

Instead, she tidies up the elfin creek that divides our properties. The creek is ephemeral and fern-spangled.

"Stop," I message her. "Go bleach your grout with a toothpick."

I throw rocks and sticks back into the creek, noticing her neat pile of "detritus": flesh-colored mushrooms that feel like skin, torn with her fingernails out of the loamy ground; oak seedlings, their tiny trunks blood-vessel thin and sappy. And an empty turtle shell.

I pull on heavy boots, laced with leather and, in my mind, hob-nailed. Red lipstick. Dark red. Yes.

She opens her front door to my pounding and blinks, but it's only a half-blink.

"Can I come in?" I ask, and then catch a whiff of a reptilian soup and an earthy, brown fragrance of fungi.

"I love company!" she sings, and fingers her kitchen cleaver.

In Nowhereland

by
John Lambremont, Sr.

In Nowhereland,
all the people are tan,
have dirty blonde hair,
grey dishwater eyes,
intonations that are monotonal,
and affects that are flat.

They complain there are no jobs,
but what jobs there are,
they refuse to take,
so they subsist mainly
on government subsidies
and old canned rations.

Their homes are few and far between,
pre-fabricated and shoddy,
and their yards large enough to be plots,
ill-defined but not disputed,
but the landscaping is spotty.

The government sends out initiatives,
often on home beautification,
but without sufficient incentive,
and in the sway of sweltering heat,
the Nowherelanders' attempts
at compliance are half-hearted,
and the results sporadic.

Their population is thinning,
so the authorities urge procreation,
but they find fornication a chore,
and prefer to lay about
on their chosen indoor spots;
orality is the norm,
and offends no one's morality,
as long as it's not too hot.

Existential Timing On Fight-of-the-Week Night

by

J. J. Steinfeld

"It's a sure thing, Danny," the man at the crowded upscale bar said to his friend.

"Sure things don't exist in this world, Gabe," Danny said, then took a sip of his third beer of the night.

"You think I would do something idiotic like throwing away money? I've bet every cent and my Rolex on this fight."

"*Even your Rolex...*"

"I'll be on easy street tomorrow, and you'll be sitting at this bar, hoping someone buys you a drink." Gabe waved his smartphone above his head and added, "You give me a thousand bucks within the next twenty minutes, and I'll place the bet for you online."

"I can't afford to lose that kind of money on some inane bet."

"Just the opposite of inane, Danny. Big-time sensible and financially judicious. You'll get five-thousand by tomorrow morning," Gabe said, and tapping his Rolex, raised his voice so everyone in the bar could hear: "Nineteen minutes left before betting closes for tonight's big Fight-of-the-Week pugilistic extravaganza."

"Five thousand, you say?"

"No risk whatsoever. I'll be pocketing ten sweet-as-heaven grand," Gabe said and ordered another drink.

Danny quickly finished his beer and left the bar, hurrying to a nearby ATM, just as three armed robbers entered, relieving all the patrons of their cash and valuables.

It is not like the movies

by
Joe Cottonwood

Caress the wrinkle, the roll of fat,

kiss the sweat,

tickle the unwanted hair.

It is not like the movies,

not really,

how you make love to a woman.

The flawless body is a myth,

the mechanism not ballet but

an awkward choreography.

It's private. It's inane.

The sensations are invisible, internal

and simply noncommercial.

More stroke, less poke.

Be slow and gentle
playful
soft in the touch
until don't.
Be messy.
It is love we are making,
not pictures.

Trash

by
Steven Carr

Every Tuesday at sunrise the garbage truck rolled noisily up the street waking Ed who always complained about the noise the garbage men made emptying the cans into the truck. After they emptied his cans into their truck and moved on down the street he would roll over and go back to sleep until his alarm clock went off.

Leaving his house and going to his car he would walk by the trash cans, always noting on Tuesdays that they had been emptied. Despite the annoyance of being awakened by the garbage collectors, their routine fit into the orderly way in which Ed led his life.

One Tuesday he woke up when his alarm clock went off and realized that he had not been awakened by the garbage collectors. As he was leaving his house he saw that his trash cans were still full of trash. He went to work feeling disconcerted, but thought that they must be running behind for some reason. After work he saw that his trash cans had not been emptied. It was after six in the evening and he knew the city waste collection department would be closed. He went to bed that night hopeful that in the morning his trash would be picked up.

Not hearing the garbage truck or the garbage men the next morning, he got out of bed after hearing the alarm and immediately went outside and saw that his trash cans had not been emptied. Before he left for work it was 7:30 and he knew the waste collection department had not opened yet. He went to work hopeful that during the day his trash would be collected. When he got home he saw that his cans were still full of trash, but again it was too late to get ahold of anyone who could tell him why his garbage hadn't been collected.

On Thursday he took the day off work and at 8:30 called the waste collection department. "My garbage wasn't collected on Tuesday and now my cans are overflowing," he told the lady who handled such problems.

"You should have called on Tuesday," the lady told him.

"I just thought they were late and I had to go to work," Ed explained.

"If you don't call the same day that your trash wasn't collected then it will be the next week before your trash will be collected," she said.

"That's inane," Ed said. "You expect me to sit around to see if my trash is going to be collected? By next

Tuesday my cans will be overflowing and draw racoons and rats and bugs."

"Call us next Tuesday if your garbage isn't collected that day," the lady said, then hung up.

The next Tuesday morning with bags of garbage piled beside the full cans of trash, Ed sat on the stoop of his house holding a rifle and dared the garbage men to not collect his trash.

WITR 9

by
R. Bremner

From above you, a walking target declared unconditional love for cosmic psychos who were cracking up when they attempted to be someone. They seek another shelter from future generations of salt in the summer rain. They also can change honey milk into light entertainment as they pick up the pace in their amazing ambulance. An ornament tried to shut up and kiss me as it went crying on a bodega run to communicate with the sun. A warning call to iron lungs caused ultimate painting of a porcelain telekinesis by a neon Indian and Annie. This time tomorrow, the industry will be off to the races to hold on to a male with royal teeth in a subterranean canyon.

(WITR is the radio station of the Rochester Institute of Technology.)

Pure Sludge
or is it?

by
Martin Christmas

Inane:

Empty. Empty.

This pert five-letter word has been around

since mid-16th century, in the Latin,

no silk, no satin.

In the Latin called inanis, empty, vain,

'quapropter locus est intactus, inanis, vacansque'

'Therefore, the place is spotless, empty, empty'.

Hard to rhyme in Google Latin so I'll abstain

and stick to English like a cunning Dane

which I am not, although there is a Manx connection.

I'll leave it there, not ramble on, or you detain.

Back to this little word, insane,

my bad . . . inane.

Some famous characters have spoke the word inane:
'A rose by any other name would seem inane'
or something more profane:
'To be or not to be inane'
Shakesword's English is hard to read.
I may have missed the point.
It's getting silly.
Inane! Inane! My kingdom for some sauce!

Time to leave this vacuous, senseless,
triffling, crass refrain
about this little word . . . 2 syllables . . . inane.

But think a moment,
just this once,
and I'm no dunce.
Without this little word
(read beyond the rhyme),
these words of mine
are serious beyond belief.

Life would be so black and white or worse,
were it not for this simple, sometimes a curse,
pure sludge word, you've gotta laugh, so lame . . .

inane.

drawling the wrong conclusion

by
Carl 'Papa' Palmer

I can't deny my origin,
my accent gives me away.
Most assume I eat grits,
love Bubba Clinton,
drive me a pickup truck,
got a black and tan coon dog,
know the latest country songs,
watch tractor pulls, WWF,
wave my confederate flag,
pinch snuff, wear bib overalls,
own a NASCAR t-shirt and
drink bunches of Blue Ribbon beer.

After hearin' my country twang,
y'all've called me a yokel, bumpkin,
hick, hillbilly, cracker and redneck,
but least I ain't trailer trash.
I done went and put my double wide
up on cement blocks years ago.

Ordinary

by
Doug D'Elia

When the rock hit him upside the head
his neck jerked, his teeth rattled, his legs wobbled,
and a trickle of blood turned pink
in the winter snow.

His headaches lasted a day or two, no more than that,
thanks to chucks of ice wrapped in a washcloth
and tinctures of iodine. He had a chestnut size bump
on his head, but other than that he was as good as new.

His mother told the relatives that she hoped
the blow would knock some sense into him.
She often apologized to people saying he was slow.
His teacher was kinder; she called him inane, a word
made

more palatable by the fact that people seldom took
        the time
to look it up. But that was before the rock, now he has
        clarity,
now colors are brighter, emotions stronger,
        intentions clearer,
and now he knows how things are going to end;

he knows that later this year his mother is going to fall
and break her hip on the ice, and in the spring
the boy who threw the rock will lose an eye in a
        rock fight.
He knows that he is going to appear on television

and that he will be the subject of more than one book,
and that he will win awards, honors, and fame,
all of which will mean little to him. He knows too
that he will carry the round, smooth rock to the top

of a mountain and throw it as far as he can,
leaning in after it, watching it transform into a pebble
that falls upon a pile of other rocks, each, from that
        distance
appearing as ordinary as the next.

Man Who

by
Martin Shaw

Wrapped in a bear hide to keep me warm, my face oozes bloodstained beard, like rusty nails. I take my helmet off and place it on the back of my matted steed. He snorts. I pat him and laugh at his energy. The air around us, it's thick with pain and fake jostling repartee from those friends who can still manage to goad.

"Enemy, can you hear me?" I shout. "If you are still there, we were much fewer than you, and like spirited youngsters we'll join together again to rave in any way we can. Your blood n' giblets, limbs and heads, screams and groans as you squirm helpless as toothless vipers, will help feed the worms."

My steed snorts again and scrapes the earth with his hoof as if drawing a finish line. I lean forward, "Yes, we have won, my friend," I whisper, "but this is only the beginning."

This Really Happened

by
Joseph Robert

"What goes through your mind sitting in such an odd place as a veterinarian psychologist's waiting room, Poochie?"

[Barking, then whining, and finally, a howl]

"Bowsy-wowsy, Poochie? Who's ready to go walkies then? Let's go buy Poochie a nice new collar with the change left over after we spend the damages I won on behalf of your emotional trauma. Remember that, Poochie? That dreadful accident when the city bus crashed into my Land Rover, where I had left you. Poor, poor, poo-poo Poochie!"

[Whimpering]

"Let's go to the department store, Poochie. After the nice-uns doggie doctor calms you down. Time for some designer labels. I'll have to lock you in the courtesy car, but don't you worry, Poochie, I've got a nice new squeaky toy here for you to chew."

[Panting]

Hail the Pen

by
Larry Lefkowitz

My boss is a pen devotee, if not a pen fetisher. On his desk a number of ballpoint pens are spread out in fan fashion, in curious contrast to a lone fountain pen. A Parker 51. The solitary pen causes me to chuckle, remembering my boss's response to Amoz Oz's revelation that he used two pens, one to write books, the second to write articles, "I use one pen; it more than does the job." Although my boss signed his more important writings with the Parker 51, he accorded pride of place in his fountain pen collection to his Parker Duofold. (He confided to me, once, that he would have loved to add to his collection the 18 carot gold-plated pen with which King Hussein signed the peace agreement between Jordan and Israel. Then Prime Minister Rabin received it in the traditional post-signing ceremonial exchange of pens, the King receiving the plastic pen Rabin used to sign. Apropos the exchange, my boss quipped, "Who says peace doesn't pay?") Soon after acquiring the Parker Duofold, he brought it to the office to show to the office staff – and holding it aloft, intoned, "I can feel, as Emile Zola felt, that 'little quivering of the pen which has always foreshadowed the happy delivery of a good book.'" His office staff vied with each other in showing inane enthusiasm for the pen. I was surprised by the pen's length, and commented on it, as the basis of my praise, which was less effusive than the ah-and-oh variety some others expressed. My boss added his own accolades. "Timeless elegance," "effortless writing, longevity, fine enough for calligraphy – try writing calligraphy with a ballpoint." Early on, my boss had recommended that I use a fountain pen: "It would improve your handwriting and, ergo, your reviews. Did not Shakespeare say, 'Let there be gall enough in thy ink.'" I chose to disregard the advice. A childhood classroom need to fill pens from an ink well – in the dying days of the breed – had left its (splattered) Rorschach stain on my psyche, even as the ink had on my hands. My traumatic association with fountain pens, I was careful to keep hidden from my boss. Never injure a man in his hobby. Especially your boss.

My boss once said that some writer, whose name he forgot, had expressed the wish to take his pen, begin a line, and finish it on the day of his death. In the silence which followed, perhaps in an attempt to 'lighten' the atmosphere, he had picked up on the pen and death connection, remarking that when soldiers came to arrest the orator Demosthenes, he asked for time to write a letter. Having filled his stylus with a deadly poison, he put it in his mouth as if considering what he wished to write, and died. "As a result of learning this," he quipped, "I stopped sucking the handles of my pens, afraid a hostile critic might ..."

The Hike

by
Kristina England

I didn't tell my mother because she'd come up with some inane response like, "I once read a story about someone that hiked in a blizzard and no one ever saw her again." When I asked where she heard it, she would quickly stumble over the white lies that I had so fondly adopted in my own life and say, "I can't remember. But it's true."

I pulled up to the path. The blizzard was more a whiteout of the already fallen snow, next batch not set to descend for another few hours. It was an unusually warm February in an unusually warm winter. New England had started to change. We would see one whammy of a winter wonderland storm and that was it. This was that storm and I had to hear what it sounded like in the woods, how the trees felt in such a state.

I climbed out and inspected the trail. If you decide to hike in a blizzard, be as careless as possible to suit the idiocy and pick a path you've never trekked before. I set out as the world whistled around me and branches crackled into heavy, scratching showers. I wore a bright orange hat and a thick coat. I doubted I had to worry about hunters or anyone for that matter. The path was mine and mine alone.

Or so I thought.

A half mile into my journey, I heard the sputtering of a motor. A snowmobile emerged from dense snow fog. The man operating it immediately stopped when he saw my hat. He squinted and seemed bewildered to see a human foot bound in the howling rage.

"Where you headed?"

A complete stranger in the middle of oblivion asking where I was headed. I could hear my mother saying, "Who's senseless now?"

After some chatter, both of voices and teeth, he advised me to turn around. He believed the storm was nearer than the weathermen had predicted and he had a long journey back through three towns. I nodded and casually turned back down the trail, though my hands shook under thick gloves. He careened away in the other direction.

I got back to my car in record speed, glancing behind me every three steps. The full storm never came. The roads remained a thin, slick mess.

A few days later, a man attacked two girls down the road from the trail. He didn't match the snowmobiler's description nor did I think he would. The snowmobiler's smiling face had not been what I was afraid of but rather what I couldn't see beyond him.

My mother called. "Did you hear? I know you hike alone. You'll be careful, right?"

I promised and as white lies go, I won't hike in a blizzard again. I like to see where I'm going although no one can prepare for every turn, whether surrounded by the ones we love or walking alone down a well-worn, heavily marked path.

Uncle Kite-Flyer

by
Chuck Augello

We were wrong to assume that he liked mushrooms.

Uncle Kite-Flyer glanced at the sliced Portobello resting on his plate and stuck out his tongue in disgust.

"Brains... it reminds me of brains..." he said, "...specifically my father's brain, which was a dark, foul, inane machine. I assume you know what he did to me..."

By now we were afraid to assume, our initial assumptions leaving us gloomy and remorseful. Uncle Kite-Flyer adjusted his collar and continued.

"When I was a boy, my father, in one of his moods, banished me to the yard with instructions to stay outside until I'd picked one thousand wild mushrooms. This was in April, the rainy season, and mushrooms were plentiful—still, one thousand remained a daunting goal. Yet I vowed to achieve it—I traversed from yard to yard filling my canvas sack with mushrooms, eager to earn my father's love and approval. Despite my precocious spirit and academic excellence, he considered me an embarrassment, an inane black mark spawned from his loins. If I called him "Father" he would cover his ears and hum Spanish madrigals until I stopped; he would only respond when referred to as 'Herr Professor'. He was ashamed of me, and I would have done anything to abuse him of the feeling. I picked and picked until my fungus-stained hands became shriveled claws and I returned home with one thousand perfect mushrooms.

"Father said nothing; he took the canvass sack, inhaled its rich moldy aroma, and sent me upstairs for my evening bath. And then, as I sat in the tub washing my weary frame, Father burst into the room and emptied the bag of mushrooms into the bath. With a large wooden spoon, he stirred the bathwater in a counter clockwise motion; from his pocket, he pulled a shaker of salt, a shaker of ground black pepper, and a single bay leaf for seasoning. I was barred from leaving the tub for exactly ninety minutes. While he gazed at the mushrooms bobbing and floating in the soap-clouded water, Father hummed one of Beethoven's symphonies, I never knew which one. Finally, he muttered, "Inane ...so inane," and I wrapped myself in a towel and ran from the bath. Only later, peeking through the half-open door, did I spy Father with his spoon eating from the tub, dunking a biscuit as he slurped spoon after spoon, sucking in the mushrooms through his pink, slender lips..."

Uncle Kite-Flyer lowered his head. "And so forgive me if I don't eat the Portobello ...and yes, I'll pass on the soup as well."

He began to weep, so we ran to our bedrooms and grabbed our kites.

"Uncle, the wind is sprightly!" we sang. We went outside, lifted our kites to the sky, and once again there was joy, our kites soaring above the trees.

We made sure that Uncle avoided the mushroom sprouting in the corner of the yard.

At the Close of the Day

by
Tracy Lee-Newman

An old widow wanted some sex before Death overtook her.

She tried to seduce the librarian, the gas man, a boy who sold dusters and tea towels, but her creaks and her creases repulsed them.

Death dealt her infection: a rattling cough.

The old widow sucked at her late husband's pipe and rethought her tactics.

She rang up old lovers and found they were dead. Looked up their sons – found them inane in care homes. One morning she woke to a numbness that pinned both her legs to the bed for the rest of the day. The next, something cold wormed through her stomach and licked at her bowels.

The old woman puffed at her pipe and told Death to be patient; she wouldn't be long.

She'd had an idea. Make a personal advert. An honest, if foolish, appeal.

Old lady would like to make love once more before meeting Reaper. No time-wasters please.

Of the seven replies she chose the youngest applicant; a trembling student whose lips kissed grey nipples to pinkness, who cupped her slack buttocks in warm, shaking hands. And after he'd left she curved a small smile round the end of her pipe, and fell into a dreamless sleep.

That night, Death brought a fever that gnawed at her bones. But she opened her dry eyes and glared at the room's tarry blackness, till dawn and the fever both broke in a haze of rose-gold.

The old widow wanted more sex.

Fed Up (IV)

by
Devon Balwit

Pretty boy sampled the product.
We can tell by his inane twitching.
His feet treadle the linoleum,
and he snuffles his jacket sleeve.
When asked, his numbers don't
add up. Pretty boy shrugs like a
dewy-eyed puppy. He doesn't
know why not, gosh and gee.
The boss semaphores and we
receive. Pretty boy's feet
need stilling. Nothing like
concrete in a bucket to give
a young man some gravitas.

Secret Men's Business

by
Irene Buckler

Our brand new *Hashimoto* barbeque stands before me in its full burnished stainless-steel glory and complete with a full-width, luxury titanium-coated cook-top, double-dipped vitreous enamel grease trap, cast-iron hotplate and four quartz technology burners. Lovingly, I stroke its gleaming exterior. However, before I can throw on my spicy marinated chicken skewers, garlic and chilli prawn kebabs and succulent basil-oregano T-bone steaks, I must first figure out how to turn it on.

The diagram in the multi-lingual owner's manual is perplexing. As I try to make sense of the inane instructions (supposedly in English), I resort to reading the *Thus, the Lighting Fat Burner* section out loud.

Must be making Part A opening lid

I open the lid and continue.

Automatic easy to Part F gases ignite.

There's nothing easy about this little lot. The labels are unclear and I am not sure if I have found Part F or Part E so I read the next bit.

If for this reason your main combustion not work, repeat 5 times

Do it five times?

Manual, power: Part C Burning grill transporting tray, fat, half burned, and then, to the right or to the left of 90mm long and ignition of match

Huh?

Making delicious for to enjoy meal on your family

Yeah right.

As I am poring over the instructions, hubby arrives and takes charge. Discarding the instruction manual, he presses and holds down the big red button on the front panel of the barbecue and it starts up – just like that!

What would I do without him?

Waiting Room

by
Anamarija Slatinec

Which celebrity dog are you? Pass

Which type of grilled cheese are you? Pass

Are you team Jen or team Angelina? What?

"How old is this thing?" I say out loud to the general area surrounding me, trying to create a jovial sense of camaraderie about the inane reading material we have been subjected to, but nobody wants to make eye contact in the waiting room of this Medical Practice.

I flip the magazine to the front cover and see August 2005. I toss it back onto the overflowing pile on the table to my left.

I check my watch. I've been in this waiting room for two hours. Now I'm circling answers on a dating quiz but I can't finish it. How long can it take to get a new prescription for my allergy medication?

I'm tapping my foot and drumming my fingers on the hand rest. The air is stale and musty like all of our collective frustration has manifested itself into the atmosphere.

I look up and see a young girl. She can't be older than 20 and she's circling questions in a quiz of her own. She must have been here a lot longer than me because I remember she was already settled when I arrived. She catches me looking at her and smiles.

"I'm Camembert and cranberry sauce"

"Excuse me?"

"The grilled cheese quiz? I got Camembert and cranberry sauce."

I see that she's holding the magazine I had tossed earlier.

"Well that's not a bad sandwich to be. How long have you been waiting now? They're terrible here right?" She shifts in her seat only slightly but enough for me to notice.

"Oh it's been a while but it's ok, I'm not in a rush and the doctors here have taken such good care of me since my surgery so I don't mind waiting."

I know it's impolite to ask so I just smile to fill the silence that's crept up on us like an unannounced house guest.

"It was a mastectomy. Breast cancer. Well hopefully in remission. That's the news I'm waiting to hear about. My name's Isabelle by the way."

She says this all with a smile on her face and not a hint of any anger or frustration. At the world, this Doctor's office or the several pointless quizzes she has surely had to complete to pass the time.

"Nice to meet you Isabelle." I suddenly feel so ungrateful and surly. I can't begin to imagine being kept waiting to find out news like that.

"Michaela Nichols?" I see the Nurse.

"That's me." I stand slowly making sure to replace the magazine in its rightful place on the table.

"I hope you don't have to endure too many more inane quizzes Isabelle." I feel silly as soon as the words leave my mouth.

"Hey, if it wasn't for these quizzes I'd never know what a kinship I share with stinky French cheese."

She's grinning and so am I.

Anne

by
Denny E. Marshall

Derrick's solo camping trip is fun until he gets lost. His phone has no signal. Batteries are low. He promised his friend Scott that he would meet him in Townville that afternoon. The last two times he made plans with Scott he was late.

After roaming around for a few hours Derrick runs into a Jim, a hiker who knows the area well. Jim guides Derrick to the closest town.

"What's the name of this town?" asks Derrick.

Jim replies, "It's called Anne."

"Ane, thanks Jim," says Derrick as he walks off to find a phone.

Under his breath Jim says, "I said Anne not Ane, you idiot."

Derek finds a phone and calls Scott.

Scott, disappointed that Derrick is late again, barks, "Where in the hell are you? What's your excuse this time?"

"I'm in-Ane," answers Scott.

The Pen from Paris:
Inane Thoughts in
the Middle of the Night

by
Ruth Z. Deming

I'd forgotten all about the pen from Paris until I cleaned between the cushions of the red couch and there it was! A transparent ball-point pen with the long tail of a phone number from the Hotel Joyce. In fact, right now I can see Sarah and me walking down the street and seeing the neon-blue sign 'Hotel Joyce'. What a relief to see it. We did so much walking. To my daughter Sarah it was nothing, like walking a block in her Brooklyn town. To me it was like walking in a marathon. My legs ain't what they used to be.

Sarah made all the travel arrangements. We wanted a decent hotel room, small was fine, since we'd spend our money on spectacular dining and touring, experiencing as much of the "City of Rain," as I called it, as was possible in only one week.

Now I keep the pen on my bedside table. At night when sleep won't come, I'll switch on the light with a 'click', pick up the pen and read the message on the side. A long tail which was the phone number. I fantasize calling the hotel, though I know not a word of French.

I'm so careless that I often misdial phone numbers. What if I accidentally dialed the private phone of the President of France? The private number no one knew.

I'd be paralyzed with fear and hang up softly.

After perhaps an hour, the sirens would wail from a mile away, then make their way down my street. They'd pound on my front door. I'd be upstairs watching television, wearing my warm polka-dot pajamas, and would have to get out of bed to answer the door, lest they use an axe to gain entry.

I'd fluff up my hair as I walk down the stairway at 3 in the morning. By now all the neighbors would be peeking out of their windows as I crack open my front door.

"Is that you?" I'd ask Lieutenant Kiersky, who gave a presentation on heroin addiction at the library. "It's me! There's been a great mistake."

He would pay no attention and on would go the handcuffs and out the door we'd go to the puzzled looks of neighbors who would wonder, "What did she do wrong anyway?"

The dark neighborhood would be lit up by the blinking red light on the cop car.

The black and white car would cruise slowly to the police station. As we'd pull into the parking loud, I'd glance up at a tall tree, where a hornet's nest, the size of a basketball net, is quietly breeding baby hornets.

"Yeah," the lieutenant would say. "We're getting it sprayed."

He'd help me out of the car and march me inside the waiting room. He'd uncuff me and ask me a series of questions, yawning as he did so.

"I'll get some coffee and drive you home," he'd say.

Berserk (or Not)

by
Alex Robertson

In previous centuries
A sickness would be pronounced
Relations 'stored away'
     as if closeted skeletons
Peculiar personality traits
Enough to gaol or asyle them
Inane of different viewpoints
Obsessed with traits and objects
Divergent thoughts and feelings
Little to relate with common stories
     of those on the outside
Chit-chat on the small points of conversation
Limited if at all present
Separated for 'our protection'...

Today we consider mental health
Differently-able like lateral thinking
Fear still habitual for the naïve
Prejudice of a different sort
Still limited career options
As the increasingly litigious
     consider what ifs
Imprisoned within society
     rather than institutionalisation
On a disability support pension

Move forward on a new generation
Accepting of a wider personality spectrum
Colourful characters on public transport
Buskers or Big Issue sellers
Instead of behind the ha ha walls
Now contained in shared accommodation
Or boarding houses
     with limited social mores
But bringing out respect in those afflicted
Wanting to remove the labels and tags
Out in the community
     medicated and benign

Gracing the greater population

Giving reasons to live

with more to offer

Than being locked away

– institutionalised

So Much for the Garden of Eden

by
Michael Mau

Draw me into the Garden of Eden. Draw me naked. Draw me with pastels. Draw me as the rocks and foliage. Draw me fat and unashamed. Draw me in two dimensions. And draw yourself, too. Pastel you and pastel me and pastel rocks and pastel water. Draw those paper birches. Draw us just at that moment—you know the one.

The moment: You have just read the poem I wrote on the bark I meticulously peeled off. You have just finished the last line, the line about the Garden of Eden. We are naked standing in my kitchen, and you have just read, "so much for the Garden of Eden." You have just told me that when you were little, your father dug up all of the grass in your backyard and created his own Garden of Eden. We are naked, and you are telling me how nothing he planted would grow, how it all died, how your father blamed the sins of the household, blamed you and your brother and your mother; how he, naked, ranted about serpents and dust; how he kicked you out of the garden and you went to live with your grandmother.

We are naked, and I have given you a poem I wrote on birch bark, and you are telling me about your father. You are speaking as your father. You are using his voice: thussing and thereforing. "So much for the Garden of Eden," you say.

Draw that moment in pastels. Draw us into that sin-fueled garden where only rocks will grow. Draw the fence you told me about, the fence on which your father painted the bushes he could never get to take root. The fence your mother had removed after they took your father away. Draw the stream he dug, the one you said he could never get to flow clear no matter what filter he attached to the fountain. The one you found him lying in, crying and cursing.

Draw just that scene just that way: you naked and me naked and the garden and the fence and the stream. Because I am not your father, and you are not your mother, and this is not the Garden of Eden, and we are not sinners, and the world isn't just so. Because I am not ashamed of being naked, because I am not embarrassed when you are naked, because those colors do not exist in nature—we just imagine them. We imagine sin, and we imagine pain, and we imagine our past with birch trees and beds, and we imagine poetry and religion and backyards and schizophrenic fathers and moments when we tell ourselves we are in love. We imagine them, and we make them real by talking about them, by writing them down, by putting pastelled pencil to paper.

So you pastel it, and I'll waste this perfectly good paper by soiling it with inane words. This will be our garden and our sin. So much for it.

The Lapse of Critical Thinking

by
Michael Marrotti

The propagation
of digital garbage
passed off as music
and the white people
who feel a need
to incorporate
the word nigga
into their shallow
vocabulary
says more than
an album worth
of music

The way the Islamists
live and die by
a primitive book
that's been antiquated
speaks more than
they're permitted
the evidence is in
the repression

Disgruntled losers
on the left
who preach about unity
are prone to attacking
those on the other side
their actions are not
making me feel like
I'm particularly wanted

Speaking of
critical thinking
the candor of this poem
is guaranteed
to sequester the audience
from the poet
diminishing the sales
of his book
and opening up the next door
for a new crude poem
that will be bypassed
by an audience
who perceives
the writer as an asshole

Awake at 4 A.M.

by
Rick Blum

Returning from midnight's bathroom sojourn
I feel the alarm clock's glow more than see it.
Outside the trees are invisible in the black void.
Not a trace of reflected light off a moon
hunkering beneath the far side of the globe.
Not a hint of impending grayness that will stir jays
and chickadees to conspicuously claim their territory.
In the silence, I slide under the covers
into a quilted cocoon, anticipating a gentle descent
back into jumbled dreamscapes. But this night,
slumber defers to insomniatic churning: Rehashing
a day of maddening inanity. Dredging up
past missteps that never fully recede into nothingness.
Imagining tomorrow careening toward chaos.
And when the domain of the mundane
has been thoroughly crissed and crossed,
when my mind, lacking an off switch,

is ready to implode, I drift unexpectedly
into an unfinished verse, or conjure up a new one
from shards of memory peeking out
beneath the turmoil. As an urgent cascade of words
unharnesses me from reality, I slowly open one eye,
half way, enough to see the edge of dawn
creeping across a skittish sky. Then close it again
to feel night tugging me back into the pit of oblivion.
Back into a world where I am perpetually 22.
Where I can walk again, and run, and, sometimes,
soar above checkerboard houses, above tangled limbs
of leafless trees, into soft, sticky clouds.
Away ... away ... away.

Float Like a Butterfly

by

Michael Webb

She will not stop talking. He is sitting there, chewing bread, watching her, filing away details so he can prove what a good listener he is. Her blouse is white and gauzy, and he can see clearly the outline of the garment underneath it, the white straps tight across her tan shoulders. What do they call that– a camisole? Something like that. He pictures it coming off her, where he would have to put his hands, where the catches would likely be, the push and pull of yes and no and I can't and we shouldn't and I will and you won't. The important thing is to keep moving, keep a small flame under her, make it so that yes is just 10 percent easier than no, and that will be that.

Allie, her name was. Alison, or Aly, or Ali perhaps. He recorded her name as Ali, so he can summon up her particular menu of dislikes and psychic pressure points and vulnerabilities under a mental image of the late boxer Muhammad Ali, a mental trick he had learned from a management book. In a way, this whole process was like a boxing match, at least the way Ali did it, the energy flow, the give and take, the chess match. Waiting for the point of weakness, and then striking there, and letting the whole edifice give way. She was talking about her sister, and he absorbed the flash of dismay that crossed her face. There is no hatred quite like the love / hate between sisters, and he knew he could use that.

The details didn't matter, although he still remembered a few of them just to show off. The feeling was what he needed, and it was coming off her in waves. She was the neglected one, the less successful one, the one who never measured up, the loser in a war nobody was fighting but her. There was always one, and she was it, and it was as if she had dropped her left, and the punch was on the way faster than conscious thought could register that there was an opening. She had fallen silent, a fine pink blush across her chest.

"I'm sorry," she says, covering the words with a laugh. "I must be boring you silly."

"Not at all," he lies, "I talk all day for work. It's a relief to hear a voice that isn't mine." Her chatter had filled the air, and the silence rolls around them.

"So...dessert?" he says. Make her say it, he thinks.

"Oh, no," she says, a hand going to her belt. "None for me. I think I'm ready to go." Letting it be her idea, he thinks, perfect, her momentum carrying them forward. He felt the click, like he had connected squarely with a golf club, or with a fist. It was over.

"Just the check," he says to their server, who hovers near his shoulder.

The Postmodern Exhibit

by
David Sklar

When Pablo Falconer announced plans for the NEW!seum, curators quivered in their sensible shoes. Who would pay to gaze at antiquities when the latest fashions, latest discoveries, latest art were there for everyone to see for the same admission?

The Museum of Natural History would survive; MOMA would be fine. But the Thomas Kinkaid Gallery feared for its life, and even the folks at the Guggenheim trembled a bit. The Pemberton sold off part of its permanent collection and made preparations to lay off half its staff.

The day the NEW!seum opened, you could hear crickets in the lobby of the Met. Inside the NEW!seum it buzzed like a nightclub so crowded you have to shout, but where nobody's listening anyway, because everyone's there to be seen.

The second day was bigger than the first. People who'd hoped to avoid the opening crowds mingled with those who came back to see how the NEW!seum staff had updated the exhibits since the day before. That night, people camped out on the street. By the third day, the whole week's admissions were sold by noon.

On Sunday morning, the week's displays were on the curb. The NEW!seum would have no permanent collection; that was their operating philosophy. If it wasn't new, it was no longer relevant. NEW!seum patrons found this honesty refreshing.

The NEW!seum didn't slash the clothes like H&M; there was no need. To people who cared, the fashions were already passé. To people who didn't, it was just inane. And neighborhood vagrants slept on park benches in clothes that cost more than your car and were about as practical as vanity plates.

By the second week, Boston was planning its own NEW!seum, as were Cleveland, Philadelphia, and L.A. The Smithsonian was considering a NEW!seum branch.

By that time, the NEW!seum was no longer new.

In the third week, attendance leveled off. By the fourth it began its decline. In the second month, the NEW!seum was only visited by irony-seekers who called it the *Nauseum.* By the third month, when the NEW!seum was threatening to close, these same patrons petitioned to have it protected as a landmark. The

NEW!seum opened for late nights and hired tour guides who wore too much black eyeliner. Still, by the end of six months, the NEW!seum had closed its doors for good.

In December, the NEW!seum was written up in the Year in Review, but by the following year people didn't recall how big it had been. By the year after, most people didn't remember it at all.

Mr. Falconer had managed his portfolio wisely. He cashed in on his put option and retired wealthy. Others went bankrupt; some lost their life savings. In that case on your left is the rope with which the general manager hanged himself. And over there, the eviction notice.

If you'll follow me this way, the next room holds our Michael Jackson collection, and on the far side of that is the Macarena exhibit. And we're walking, we're walking....

The Look

by
Abha Iyengar

Anirban showed me a photograph and said I was to dress and pose like the woman in the photograph. This woman was slim to the point of emaciation and wore a white dress that fell straight down from her shoulders. Her skin was a deathly white. She held two white doves in either hand and stood at three-quarters, facing the camera, holding the doves as though they were porcelain instead of birds that could very well fly away. There was no sign of anxiety in her stance or on her face. Her short and very black hair accentuated her whiteness. The backdrop was also white. Just behind here were the fine leaves of a tree, and they were the only black in this very white photo, apart from her hair.

I raised my dark, manicured eyebrows. I raised my manicured hand, a flourish of brown fingers with red nail paint. My gold bracelets winked in the light. I gave Anirban a look to freeze him into a similar ghost-like pallor like that of the woman in the photograph.

"What an inane idea, Anirban!" I exclaimed, arranging the three layers of gold necklaces that adorned my throat and fell heavily into my heavier bust. The long danglers of gold and pearl fell from my ears and grazed my smooth brown shoulders, revealed by the short red brocade sleeveless blouse. My sari of yellow tissue draped around my heavy curves, which made many an Indian male sigh when I appeared on screen. And this Anirban, a young fledgling of a photographer, wanted me to be like that woman. A thin walking stick in white, holding doves in her hand!

I turned to Picku, my parrot in his cage, as he cackled after me, "What an inane idea, Anirban!"

"True, Picku, true," I said, and gave Anirban another look. "Do you see me?" I asked him.

He nodded, not the least perturbed. His golden brown skin, much lighter than mine, did not pale, despite my withering look. "But Madam, everyone sees you like this. As you see yourself. All brown and gold and…"

I raised my hand again. "I know, and that is what they know, and love." I pulled my sari tighter to accentuate my curves. "Take my photograph as I am. Maybe I can hold Picku… just to get a bird in the photo…make it a bit different…" Picku's green would work well with my colours.

He walked up to me, and I admired his taut young looks. I wasn't that old either, but ten years in the industry had aged me fast. "May I?" he said, and when I nodded, he opened up my hair. It fell down my back. He asked me to remove my jewellery, then my make-up.

He was undressing me. My heart fluttered like the wings of the doves in the cages around us. As I melted in the white fire lit with his passion, the look he wanted was what he held in his hands.

In Ane

by
Dimple Shah

Let me tell ya a little secret.

I'm in Ane.

I know it sounds weird. What does it mean, to be in Ane?

Honestly, I still don't know. I'm kinda slow that way, always have been. Most folk call me stupid, and retard, and stuff. It used to make me angry. Now it just makes me sad.

I always felt there was something more to life, but it was only recently that I found out what it was. I was helping a woman in the supermarket where I work. She wanted to know where the plum tomatoes were. I told her that was confusing: did she want plums or tomatoes? Because they're in different places and if she wanted plums and I took her to where the tomatoes were kept, she'd get mad but if she wanted tomatoes and I took her to where the plums were kept–

She interrupted me. "You're in Ane, you know that?"

"What?"

"In Ane! Totally in Ane!"

She walked off, leaving me wondering what she meant. It took me a while to realize she meant I lived in a special place.

Living in Ane is pretty much like living anywhere, it all looks the same. Not many people know that I live there. Those who do let it slip out sometimes. "Don't go on with your in Ane talk," they'll say, or, "Cut out that in Ane gibberish, will you?" They seem almost angry when they say that. I guess it's hard for them to keep pretending all day long. I try to make them feel better. I go closer to them and whisper, "It's a secret." And wink. For some reason that always seems to make them more mad.

There must be other in Ane folk, but I don't know who they are. It'd sure be nice to meet them. I once heard that blondes are in Ane. That got me really excited. All them beautiful blondes, like Samantha Price? I went up to her once, after History class, and told her we should get together and talk about what it's like being in Ane. She called me a dweeb and a turd, but I know she was just pretending, in case someone was listening.

My cousin Mark was visiting us last summer. He's always been real nice to me, but when he heard my secret, this sad look came over his face.

"Come here, Mikey. I want you to see this".

It was a big fat book, a dictionary, and he had it open on a specific page.

"Inane," I read. "Absurd, unintelligent, nonsensical."

"That's not the same thing!" I yelled. "I live in Ane, that's a place, okay? And it's spelt differently and all, can't you see? And it's not absurd or nonsensical. It's wonderful and exciting and special. *I'm* special!"

"Oh Mikey," he sighed.

I'm right. I *know* I'm right.

Besides, it could be worse. I could be like them other folk.

I could be in Sane.

The Hare

by
Susan Doble Kaluza

Porcupine ugly, its fur
bloody and spiked
like it'd been dragged through
the rain by something large
jawed and angry, it hunches
half hidden against a sawed
off pine log I keep on the porch
to match the deck, which shakes
in the wind and creaks when
you lean into it. But the hare,
its eyes wild and far too dark
to disclose what kind of life
must be buried there, is something
you might find on a frozen
mid morning in Greenland—
your own life the far off
emptiness you imagine

it's made of—an entire island
of dwarfed vegetation
and windblown sand and your soul
in the murky midst of it like the body's
cells spin doctoring multiples
of themselves to keep from dying,
and you think to survive, all you'd need
is that inane fear firing
in the brain of a creature
appearing to have come from
nowhere but which is now
bloodless and grey as scrubbed
shale against the neighbor's
basement wall, straining the hard
clots into its mouth as one would ring
out a mop to disperse the pain.

Next to Te Uru

by

Piet Nieuwland

Remodelling Titirangi hotel, blue mountain guest house into a gallery exhibition, then into a faux Turkish café echoing the exotic middle-east with the blood spilled at Galipolli, codifying the colonial blue while the café down the road laments this weekend buzz, the rush and clamour of tourism, the weary but beaming staff. Through the alcove a table of Aucklandites, young, urbane, well dressed, the men's haircuts short sided leaving a heavy mop top, the women young chatting smiling tanned. Conversation fluid as a shaken molasses or a fizzing soda pop gaggle and drops dripping over the tables, fountains in tidal surges around the chairs, filling the room in a flood of nuances exchanges, deep meaningful discourse, the frames and mirrors, seeing part of the room, pieces, fragments of people, the girl in orange, the man in black, the selfies of selfies, the waitresses, grinning again with busy efficiency, greeting the cake open from the platter, and disappears in a sweetish fruity pale scented gesticulation of swallows, the pieces crumbled and sliding over the olfactory surfaces. Are the people satisfied with the result of their craving, the culture they join with their friends and lovers, families and acquaintances, the people they know but never know, the languages they occupy, signalling and reciprocation, the coy and the gathering trust, how much we reveal through that gap of knowing, and not knowing our assumptions, however inane, meaningless, unfounded, they might be.

Keep Moving

by
Ashley Morrow Hermsmeier

It happened while walking to Study Hall after yet another "incident" with Ms. Ranis. Today—even though it was under her breath and even though hardly anyone heard it and even though it's completely true—Sidney was sent out of class for calling Ranis a bitch.

What did it matter? Even if she said nothing all day long, someone would find something to pin on her. All the Someones see her purple hair and heavy eyeliner and thigh tattoos—that's right, *thigh* tattoos, so what?— and say things like, "That girl looks *all* used up"—like Ms. Ranis did last week. The Someones think: *We lost the battle with this one*, and: *Another hopeless case*, because what can they do for a 17-year-old with a dad in prison and a mom with too many kids and too many bills? It's the same thing they do for all the other kids with missing fathers and broken mothers—kids who have to babysit their younger siblings so Someone can take an extra day shift at the parking garage. It's the same thing they do for the kids with undiagnosed dyslexia or ADHD or IBS or whatever: A whole lot of nothing that sounds like, *we've reported this to the state.*

So when the state can't make dad stay, and when the state can't make mom leave the gin in the cupboard, and when the state tries to put the younger siblings in foster care, well, it's then that big sisters and lasher-outers like Sidney get sent to Study Hall to write a fucking reflection.

She was done reflecting—done looking back—except that, looking forward didn't make much sense either. What did she have to look forward to? Not prom. Not graduation. Not a full-ride scholarship to the school of her choice like ASB president slash valedictorian slash "you-can-be-anything-if-you-just-dream-it," Kelly Caldwell (and that's for damn sure).

She crossed the quad toward the office. The sun bright and unfiltered above made her shadow seem darker somehow. Her head bobbed up and down like a kid untethered, like she had something worth bobbing about—and that's the moment it happened.

She froze mid-step beside the dark shade of the Library.

She leaned just a hair, just a sliver of an inch, and her shadow—*for real, no lie*—stretched toward the shade of the Library, and the Library's shadow stretched toward hers in return. And, somewhere in the fragment of light between the two, the shadows fused together in some kind of illusory handshake. She leaned the other way and her shadow took her shape again. She remembered Someone at some point had told the class that light could bend. But, what could shadows do? She leaned again and, yes, her shadow stretched itself with what looked like the very same longing she felt.

A voice called from across the quad, "Keep moving!"

Ranis stood outside the classroom, arms crossed.

Sidney walked on far enough from the shade of the building that when she stood straight, so did her shadow; when she tilted just-so-much, the two shadows reached for each other. There had to be something to this. Maybe it would leave her—it seemed so easy for everyone else to leave. Or maybe she could go with it, could walk in another dimension. Maybe she could become whatever she was before she became a life— when it was just darkness. She closed her eyes and tried to feel the pull of her shadow. Of another life. Of anything at all.

Nothing.

It all felt the same in the light and in the dark. As she knew too well, bad shit happened in both.

Sidney kept moving, alright. Kept moving past Study Hall, the administration building, the flagpole, the parking lot, the marquee flashing, "Talent Show Tonight @ 6!" She moved from shadow to shadow and no one stopped her to ask: *Just where, exactly, do you think you're going?*

Saint Agnes

by
Ruth Sabath Rosenthal

who knew the truth of her
would grow to poetic heights of fancy & myth
that her dreams of the man of her dreams
would have him marrying her
and living in connubial bliss ever-after

— the stuff of maidens' dreams — fantasy
of the highest order prompting inane ritual:
lovelorn maidens walking naked backwards
to bed (their hymens intact) that right after
having devoured an excess of dumb cake*

who knew truth of her would inspire men
to dream of dancing virgins clad in white
pure as driven snow — men of all color & creed
inspired by not only her
but also of multiple virgins like her

she who at age twelve so desired love

of only the son of God

she whose innocence was subverted by a miscreant

so influential he'd have her burn at the stake

for refusing him but for the grace of God

and yet despite that

grace of God mysteriously

her throat was cut her hymen still intact

in point of fact that

being what grew martyrdom to legendary heights

* A cake made on an auspicious day (St. Mark's Eve (April 24th), St Agnes Eve
(January 20th) Midsummer's Eve or Halloween) with numerous ceremonies,
by spinster maids, to discover their future husbands. The name may derive
from the middle English 'doom' meaning 'fate' or 'destiny'.
http://www.foodsofengland.co.uk/dumbcake.htm

A poem for you

by
Donna Krause

I'm going to write you a sweet poem
One that you'll never forget
Each word will be dripping with
Sweet nectar,
My sentences will make
Your spring flowers more fragrant
And appealing to your eye
I'll tell you that my love
For you
Will never die
It will live on like
The tides of the ocean
And the sands of the beaches
I'll tell you
That you're beautiful
Sweet as an inane
Honeysuckle bush

In full bloom
I'll whisper in your ear
And give you
Sweet lovely kisses
That will surely
Bring a tear to your eye
I'll bring you angels
That will fly above you
And protect you
As you slumber
You will call me your sweetheart
And grow to love me
Looking at me
With those luscious
Blue eyes
We'll make children
Under the sleepy moon

Growing old…
Remaining to be
Sweethearts
Dying together
In an embrace…

Just one thing…
I've not met you yet

Exploding Star

by
Mark Govier

The road out of town is still not repaired. This has nothing to do with that exploding star 2 years ago. The crops grow, the factories produce, business prospers, my contract's even been extended. I eat, drink, wallow in debauchery. I was a cleaner at the State Astronomy Institute. I'd been an astronomer's sub-assistant, until I was caught doing lines in the back-office.

Then, that stupid star, Gyrus 1, 5 light years away, decided to collapse. Not expand, as had been expected, it blew up. They said it was 5 billion years old, with 1 billion to go before a period of slow expansion. But what do astronomers really know?

I was sitting alone, in the ancillary workers' cafeteria, in the sub-basement. It was 3 am. I'd nearly finished my shift, was reading one of those shit free papers. Suddenly, a bright light appeared, continued. Had I been upstairs, as an astronomer's sub-assistant, I'd have been fucked. I heard the wailing from above.

'I can't see, I can't see, help me, help me…'

I hid under a table, closed my eyes.

By 6 am, the bright light had moved onto other lands. I went upstairs, into the Observatory. Medical staff were everywhere. The night shift astronomers sat numb, despairing, too shocked to speak, or cry. They were all blind. I managed to get out. While waiting for the bus, I noticed the animals in the farm next door baaing and mooing, all blind. The News Feeds said everyone must stay indoors, until advised otherwise. Opportunists roamed the streets, breaking and entering, stealing anything they could. I saw the police shoot a couple. I stayed in my flat, covered the window with masking tape.

The light returned for 1 more night. Then stopped. The Astronomy re-opened the following week. One of the astronomers told me not even a small speck of Gyrus 1 was left.

Side effects soon became known. Few baby sheep, calves, piglets were born in the months after. Sterility! It was the same with us. Everyone who'd been directly exposed, like the night shift astronomers, was sterile. It was the end of life, as they knew it. News Feeds said many others had been blinded from looking at the exploding star through dark glasses, including 2 of the Astronomy's sub-assistants. Thanks to them, I got my old job back. No more mopping piss on the floors and seats, cleaning lumps of shit clinging to the bowls.

I look out my window. In the distance I see green fields. The sun is going down. Beautiful...

Facial Pareidolia and the Judgement of Flowers

by

Alison J. Fish

Iris rocked. Her eyes wily, like flattened keyholes. Her chin puckered. The wallpaper had changed. Perhaps she was just seeing it differently. Twenty years without an update. Not even a lick of paint. Nothing revamped. Boldly familiar, woodlice scuttled. Iris aimed, squirting rat poison in powdery puffs. "That will see 'em," she muttered.

Iris knew a little about chemical imbalance. Nightly she mixed a rum punch. Sleeping pills were followed by morning caffeine, sweet with saccharine. Hair of the dog, she could never get her tongue around the expression, but a tipple at dawn sounded heavenly. Being breathalysed tipsy was surely a sackable offence, along with the whopping deterrent of a prison sentence.

Iris no longer worked, nor drove. Jim, the neighbour, remarked that the death penalty was abolished in 1998.

Iris gripped the handle of her pink feather duster. Her home was too cluttered for DIY. She liked her heirlooms and had no desire for modernity or doses of TLC. The garden was passable. Thanks to Jim. Iris could remember laying back on the decking with him, drinking and counting bizarre pictures in the clouds. But having faces in her wallpaper was a disturbance. It couldn't continue. "Worse than gremlins!" she growled.

Iris pulled the doors of her side cabinet open even wider and then stumbled to close the curtains. She had to hide the faces, the staring judgemental gaze of the yellow tulips. Their eyes blinked innocently. But their mouths, where the turquoise stems and sepals met, were ominously zippered, stitched to gag.

The diagonal strip of flowers, shining from the embossed tulip wallpaper, was moving. These hallucinatory optical illusions created faces with inane smiles of a ghostly knowing. Iris arose. She took a step closer to the wall. Her cheek pressed firmly against it, "Who asked you?" Iris waggled a ringless finger, then waited for their choral reply.

Later it was Jim who tucked her in, emptied the vases and poured hot milk in a plain glass.

The following day, she faced her shrink, crossing her ankles, twisting her forearms and wrists around in a stretch. "So what's up, doc?" Sometimes she didn't even know if she'd spoken out loud. Here the walls were plain.

The fibrous scratchy nib, on premium bond, filled the space with a splatter. Boxes were ticked. "Another signature, here and here." They knew it may come to this. Iris was too far along to realise the consequences of self-medication, prescription drugs and anti-depressants.

Her name was an exaggerated flourish, barely contained, imprisoned in the formality of the permission box.

In her nightmares, physicians approached. Her arms were lifted and the jacket fastened. Ready for further observation, Iris was led to a poorly decorated room. It needed fresh paint or some decent wallpaper. Her floral patterned anorak filled with sunny daffodils was left on a coat hook. After a barrage of tests, she glared sideways, just as the daffodils raised their heads in unison and grinned, "So you've sided with them, huh?"

Inane on the Train

by
Mark Hudson

On Saturday, I went to a poetry workshop at
Harold Washington library in Chicago, with a
distinguished De Paul University professor as the
workshop facilitator. There were about twenty
people, and you sent your poem a month in
advance, and it was critiqued anonymously.
A lot of people's poems got ripped to shreds,
but mine got great reviews. One man even said,
"Whoever wrote this must be an intelligent
individual." I was flattered.

On the way back to Evanston, I got on
the train at the el stop Jackson, and these two
kids in their early twenties (I say kids because
I'm forty-six. Some might say I'm a kid, too!)
got on, and they had coffee in hand. One kid
had an ice creamy coffee in his hand, and as
he sat down, the cup fell on the ground, and
the contents went all over the floor of the

train. He took a napkin, cleaned it up, and shoved it under the seat.

It took me a few moments to realize the kids were either drunk, high, or both. These girls got on, and one girl seemed to be laughing at what geeks they were. The kid tried to talk to her, and she said,
"Do you guys party?"
The kid said, "Yeah."
And then the girls got off around Wrigley Field, so I assumed they were baseball groupies. When they got off, the one kid said to the other kid, "You should've got their phone numbers."
"I was close, dude."
They maybe exchanged three sentences! Ah, youth!

Then a mother was getting off the train with a six-year old kid who was rapping about mashed potatoes.
One of the high kids said, "Don't you wish you could be a kid again? Life was so simple then! My parents spoiled me so much! Every Christmas I got so many toys!"
I grinned inwardly. A kid wishing he was a kid? Ha!

Their conversations went on, about hoping
to find a job, since their unemployment was running
out, then they got off in Rogers Park to buy another
bag of dope.

As I stood on the Howard platform, I thought,
"Those kids were stupid!" Puffing myself up with pride,
like I had just got praised for my poem by a De Paul
professor, and these kids were just uneducated, hopeless
dope fiends, going nowhere. The one kid even said
he got arrested, and his dad saw his mug shot on-line.

But when I thought about it later, God gave
me some humility. I realized I was once that age, and
I was probably just as befuddled and as confused
at that age. And with a building inspection coming
up, I'm freaking out and in my mind, I've already
failed and I've been tossed out on the streets. I
think the saying is "Pride comes before a fall."
Well, when you hit rock bottom, the only way is up...

We'll Meet Again

by

Neil Laurenson

Dad had disappeared and Mum was living on an island where people were outnumbered by puffins. University holidays were therefore spent with my grandparents. I got a weekend job in a kitchen in an old people's home to pay for beer and microwave meals. On my breaks, I played the piano in the large dining room. Initially, I didn't care if anyone said anything about the repetitive major chords or inane arpeggios. Half of the residents had dementia and all of the staff hated me. One of them was particularly evil – a young, bug-eyed sadist called Emma, who liked to report me to the manager for not doing my job. She once caught me watching the football with Harold (after I had finished my shift) and from then on convinced herself and everyone else that I wasn't bothered. They believed her, despite me regularly showing them my flaky, red Fairy Liquid hands. My eczema was so bad, I could barely see the black keys on the piano, though it didn't make any difference anyway. On my last day before term, I was making my usual racket when I heard someone scream, "Shut up!" It was Gladys. Fat Gladys. Gladys who had three breakfasts and four dinners. Gladys with the tree trunk legs and permanently purple face. I stopped and went to see her.

"Are you OK, Gladys?"

"Was that you? It was awful."

I was genuinely hurt.

"But I thought you liked the piano. What about that chap with the keyboard who plays Vera Lynn songs?"

"Yes, Vera Lynn — on a *keyboard*."

"They're the same thing."

"No, they're not. Stop talking to me and make me a cup of tea."

I was about to tell her that I don't make tea, but that would only have confirmed to the sentient ones that I was a lazy student. I made her a cup of tea, with two teaspoons of spit, and committed myself to learning 'We'll Meet Again'.

Back at uni, I spent every night I would have been in the bar on the piano in the common room. I received a whole different level of abuse, but this time no one disputed my work ethic. Four hours, seven nights a week.

I almost couldn't wait for my first shift back. As soon as it was break time, I rushed to the stool and began to play as if I was in the Royal Albert Hall. It was a near perfect performance, as indeed it should have been. No one applauded, but the silence was all I was after. Time to boast to Gladys. I went to see her but she wasn't in her chair.

"Where's Gladys?" I asked Margaret. She stroked her beard and about ten seconds later said:

"She's dead."

"You won't be meeting *her* again!" laughed Harold, wetting himself.

Fear of the Mould

by
Leilanie Stewart

Fear of the mould is the inane fear of fear itself. Fear is the smell of decay; a worry that the mould will catch up with you, that the spores of the old place will infest the new. Is everything polluted? Contaminated?

Fear is that spreading sewage behind the walls — the brown speckled patterns on whitewashed walls. Only this time, it's in you. And even though you cleaned the four walls that boxed you in, even though you scrubbed them with a sponge and bleach, you fear the rot has already set in and will come back. You've moved on, run away — but you haven't escaped. You can smell the mould in your clothes and hair. Yet it doesn't taint those around you; only you.

The four walls of the new courtyard should give you safety, but they don't. You're alone with the fear. It has desensitised you. All the smells in this new place are unfamiliar and so you feel detached; alien. You cook, you spray air freshener, but you can't shake off the old, damp smell of lingering, festering evil underlying it all.

You walk the busy streets of the big city. Though the people pass you by, you feel a fleeting desperation; you want to shake off this rot but you can't. Talking about it to someone gives you temporary relief, but still the fear crawls. It seeps under the surface, the same as in the old place. The old place is empty now, but you had to go back to clean it through contractual obligations; even now it lures you back. As you cleaned, you saw the blackness on the sponge; the fetid stains on your hands. You worked without any clothes on so it wouldn't taint them, but it didn't help. You wore a surgical mask filled with scented oil, but still the death-spores stung your eyes.

The mould creeps into your mind at night and leaves you in a cold sweat. It trickles into your guts, making them squirm, filling you with the gas of pain. You know what the mould means – so many bad events happened in that place, so many evil memories that slipped behind the dreaded walls, wove themselves into the fabric of the building.

The escape doesn't feel real for you. You feel that the new place has the air of holiday about it; artificial, unreal. The fear is that it is all a dream, that the new life will be whipped from under you and you will be back at the old place. Back in the rot. Unable to leave the stench.

The rot is a fear of the monster within you; a conjugation of the evil that they inflicted upon you, and your own powers of perpetuation. The mould threatens to rear its ugly head inside your own soul, to eat you from the inside out.

But you are on a high floor now in the new place. These four walls of the courtyard can set you free. By facing the evil, instead of denying it and letting it fester, you have shed the rot. The clothes no longer smell. The air smells of the home you have made. You have left the monsters behind – you will not become the next generation of rot. You will not continue the cycle of fear. You can feel the wings on your back. The window opens towards an endless sky. Your wings will take you to a new beginning.

A Squeal from My Automobile

by
Embe Charpentier

I named my yellow Smart Car 5 'Chiquita'. As Shakespeare said in *Midsummer Night's Dream*, "Though she be little, she is fierce." A self-driving car isn't so surprising, but Chiquita and her sisters are the least expensive self-driving cars in the country.

When my manager at the cubicle farm cut my hours in half after Christmas, I focused on keeping a roof over my head. I remembered how to love ramen noodles, those stiff spirals that staved off starvation while I studied drama. The heat in the apartment was set at a bone-chilling 62. But there was Chiquita. I called the car dealer to explain the late state of my payments.

"It's just a temporary setback, Mr. Brant."

"Setbacks have consequences, Miss Carter," he replied, then hung up.

One stiff icicle of a morning, I ran down the stairs. I couldn't be late for my semi-job soothing customers who needed — yes, needed — a giant rotisserie that doubled as an indoor barbeque. I pressed Chiquita's start button. "Good morning, Aisha," she said. "We're going to the dealership on Main Street."

"No time for maintenance, Chiquita. The job's at 1500 Industrial Park Place."

Her flat, female voice was usually so damned amiable, yet suddenly I was reminded of Hal in the movie *2001*. "I'm locking the doors and taking you to 755 Main. You *do* want to make your car payment, don't you?"

Tiger-footed rage. Yes, a full Shakespearean tantrum waited stage left. "Chiquita! I can't pay for you if I don't work!"

"Aisha, I'm repossessing myself. If you can't pay, perhaps Mr. Brant can interest you in a," and I was sure I heard a wounded sniffle, "used, non-self-driving model."

Oh, I could still drive myself. "I want you to put the settings on manual control."

"I don't think you should do that."

Infuriated, I turned off the self-driving function with a few flips of switches. Life was like the old days, when humans commanded machines like Henry V sent men into battle. "Once more unto the breach," I mumbled as I put my lazy right foot on the gas pedal. My knuckles ratcheted around the wheel. Escaping from the tiny, snowbank-bordered parking space took me a couple of forwards and backs, but my tires hit the street.

Then, mechanical collusion. My phone chimed. Eyes down for less than two seconds and smash. The guy in the old non-self-driving car who dented my passenger's side door honked at me to pull over. Again, 212 degrees Fahrenheit.

"Why didn't your car react?" he asked.

From *As You Like It*: "I do desire that we may be better strangers." But you shouldn't quote Shakespeare while exchanging insurance information.

I surrendered when I sat back down. "Self-driving mode. And I'm sorry."

"I accept your apology." Chiquita revved her engine. Repo ahead.

Did a mere machine outsmart me? I'd like to think not, but honesty is surely the cruelest turn of the screw.

Compartmental

by
LaVa Payne

"I tell you I have been in the glove compartment for three days now!"

The exacerbated little voice rambled. "And if you had not pulled her over to ask for her license and registration, I might have died in there."

"Ma'am, I am going to need you to step out of the vehicle slowly."

"Am I under arrest officer?" The plague of being placed in handcuffs was horrendous. "This, this little man is clearly delusional, and I have never seen him before in my life, I swear it!" I made a cross-my-heart motion across my chest. It made little difference to the officer: he unbuttoned the holster to his gun.

"I repeat, step out of the vehicle and place your hands in the air slowly."

My mind was racing a thousand different directions. *Who is this wee little man, and how in the world did he get in my glove box? Who had put him there? And why was he telling the officer that I had locked him in there for three days?* The entire idea of it was perplexing me, and I wrinkled my brow.

"Look, look officer, she is making a face at me and she is going to..." his little voice trembled and was very believable.

But enough was enough.

"Shut up!" I said. My words were harsh.

At that moment, the officer jerked the car door open and threw me to the ground. At which out of the corner of my eye, I could see the little man rubbing his palms together. I could not see him, but I could definitely hear him.

(I will be fine now officer, thank you so much for rescuing me! I need to call my family and let them know I am alright, the little voice cooed.)

I could see the lights flashing as I felt the last latch on the handcuff.

click.

The officer pulled me to my feet and firmly tucked me into the back of his police car.

As the officer sat behind the wheel, I asked, "What about my car keys? Won't someone steal my car?"

He just smirked, "Not if the wrecker service gets here first."

There was a short pause—only a pause.

"What about the little man in my glove compartment? What are you going to do about him?"

silence

"Female, traveling North on Highway 14, found half-naked behind the driver side air bag, speaking in riddles and talking to a little man she claimed lived in her glove compartment."

Straw Man

by
Tom Fegan

Judge Emma Carlson pushed back her bifocals from the edge of her nose with a stiff forefinger as she studied the teenage youth standing before her: Jon Peters, the only son of a wealthy Dallas family. His stooped posture straightened at the behest of his defense attorney Prescott Jones. Jones was the best money could buy. I witnessed his manipulative legal strategies with disdain in my two decades as a Dallas County Bailiff.

Quiet intensity paralyzed the courtroom in anticipation of Carlson's ruling against the underage felon for the unremorseful vehicular manslaughter of three other teens while he was driving under the influence of pot and booze. Peters had rocketed through a stop sign and crashed into a passing vehicle killing the trio. They were returning home from a movie.

"Ten years probation," she clicked through her dentures and pointed, "You must seek counseling, engage in community service and attend A.A. meetings for the duration of your probated sentence.

Furthermore, you cannot imbibe alcohol or recreational drugs. You will be tested regularly!" Gasps of shock whistled from witnesses, paired with sobs of family members of the lost teens, reeled painfully throughout the courtroom. Carlson hammered her gavel, "Order!" I face the angered crowd to keep them still.

"Do you understand this?" she asked Peters. He responded with a silent nod. Officers escorted him and Jones out between the scathing onlookers. My stomach knotted as I recalled the statement of defense at the young man's arraignment, "Jon Peters is not accountable for his actions due to his ignorance of responsibility. He is a product of his environment and has been raised in wealth with servants, tutors, as well as attending private schools and therefore the circumstances have lead to his ignorance of his responsibility as a citizen. He is a victim of Affluent Disorder and therefore not guilty of this grievous error of judgment."

Jones transformed Jon Peters into a Straw Man, a legalese term in which an obviously guilty person is presented as innocent and goes free. Peters skipped to Puerto Vallarta where extradition is futile in most cases. He stayed with his mother at the family condo. A figurative thumbing of the nose to the judicial system, I felt. "He will return," declared Judge Carlson.

Leafmeal

by
Philip Kobylarz

Into a nondescript cardboard box, they packed what remained of her life since she wasn't one for owning things and due to her great age, although she would argue that there wasn't much great about living ninety-six years, she didn't really need much more than her prayer books, her many and ornate crucifixes that she worshipped and even kissed as if they were secret idols, her myriad votive candle holders, useless and come to think of it cheap religious knickknacks that others sent her when she entered into those last years of the ill weather of her diminishing health, the days, the months, seasons she would sit in her wheelchair, that she despised more than sin itself, and through the sliding glass door that her daughter resolutely cleaned each day and then shined with yesterday's newspaper, she would watch the every movement and behavioral pleasantries of a local, temporary flock of birds—mostly sparrows, robins, grackles, a intermittent jay—the most common of commons, and how she would talk of the worms they would try to loosen from the ground or the long gulps of water they'd take from the ashtray she would fill with cold water for them when she could get around better, because she collected these, from a Europe she never cared to return to, to hold the thin stalk of ash of her daily menthol cigarette that no one, not even she, knew why she smoked at the same time of each and every day and then dumped into the fenced off rectangle of the garden in hopes that from it, in it, something useful and beautiful might grow.

The notice

by
Matthew Harrison

I'm standing outside a Japanese restaurant on Hong Kong Island – I won't say exactly where, it's a little secret of mine! – and I'm reading the notice on the wall. It has a cartoon of a waitress crying, with the caption, 'Please excuse us for the deficiencies in our service'.

Now, I am rather particular about words – I'm an English teacher here – and when the actual waitress comes, I say, "Your service hasn't *got* any deficiencies – at least not yet!" I explain that I have been to her restaurant before, and the service has been fine. There is every prospect that it will be fine this time.

The waitress laughs, and gives me the menu.

I order, but I'm still thinking about that notice. Do they mean it putatively – 'If we *should have* deficiencies in our service...'? But the definite article seems, well, too definite for that. And there's the tears as well.

Come, I say to myself, it's just a cultural clash – a Chinese manager trying to translate Japanese sensibility into English. But the thing nags me, particularly since my meal comes without any deficiencies at all.

Finally, I call the manager. He comes over, a mild and obliging sort of fellow, and I tell him my problem. It takes a while, but when he gets it, he smiles and thanks me. It is just to be polite, he says.

"Then you should say, 'for any deficiencies you might find', or something like that."

"Yes, sir, very good," he says, looking harassed now. "Please accept our apologies. If there is anything sir would like? Some Kirin beer?" He is actually sweating.

Then one of the waiters shouts, *"Irasshaimase!"* as a guest comes in. The other waiters repeat it, and in the hubbub the manager hurries off. The waitress brings me the promised Kirin.

I sip it, mulling the issue. Then I have it. Of course! That anthropologist chap I was reading the other day, Sapir-something – he says a language embodies the world-view of the people speaking it. That fits perfectly with what I know of Chinese – it's short on tenses. And goodness knows what they do in Japanese! The manager lives in a world where unactualised deficiencies are solidly present: he's dodging them all the time. That's why the Chinese believe in demons. It all fits!

I'm a bit of a philosopher, you see, and as I finish the Kirin – no deficiencies there! – my duty becomes clear. I pay the bill, and march past the other tables. I see the manager turn in alarm. But he needn't worry, no demons here!

I reach the door. There's that notice, with its offensively definite article. I take out my pen, ignoring the cries, the rushing feet. I strike through, 'the', and scrawl in, 'any'. The manager screams.

I turn to reassure him. But the restaurant has disappeared, and in its place a swirling mist, huge menacing forms...

I Have a Window in My Home Office

by

Paul Beckman

My home office window overlooks my back yard which is mostly grass except for a lone tulip tree. Tulip trees grow tall and straight and I often think I want to take a level from my garage workbench and hold it against the tree to see if the bubble centers but I always forget when I'm in my garage. When I'm in my office thinking I should do it I never would leave my office for that alone. Maybe I'm putting it off so I can think about it without knowing because once I use my level (it's a three-foot metal one), then I'll know for certain and the tulip tree won't hold my interest as much even though I'll still think it's beautiful and wonder at its straightness—even if it's not level straight but only eye straight.

The tulip tree roots are under the lawn not like some trees whose roots show from the trunk of the tree and then dip into the lawn. This is much neater and in keeping with a straight tree to my way of thinking.

I keep my lawn at one and a half inches and that way I only have to cut it every other week. Some of my neighbors are three inchers because they like to see the grass wave in the breeze, which I have to admit is attractive, but that means they have to mow every week or it gets away from them and it makes their lawn look like they don't care about it which isn't the case.

There's a bright green rectangle on the north side of the tulip tree which is right over my septic tank. When the sun is out and bright it looks as if I Photoshopped that rectangle and I imagine doing the same to the rest of the yard so it would all be a bright green but that's not realistic.

Overall I'm pleased with my yard and since the lawn is surround by woods I can barely see my neighbor's house and therefore he can barely see mine. That's the benefit of one acre zoning. Some people prefer two acre zoning and that's all right with me but then you have to pay taxes on that extra acre which almost no one uses unless they cut a path through it so their kids can ride their ATVs around. One acre's not enough if you want your kids to have ATVs which no parent in their right mind should want their kids to have.

I just noticed a couple of dandelions off to the side of the yard and I'm going to go out now and pull them out by their roots. They're weeds, after all, and I don't want my eyes to look out from my home office when I'm working away and see weeds. It would be very distracting. I think I'll grab my level from the garage on my way to pull those little bastards.

Authors

Chuck Augello

lives in New Jersey (USA) with his wife, dog, two cats, and several unnamed squirrels that inhabit the back-yard. His work has appeared in *One Story*, *Juked*, *Hobart*, *Smokelong Quarterly*, *A Lonely Riot*, and other fine journals. He is an editor at *Cease, Cows*, and contributes to *The Review Review*. He also publishes *The Daily Vonnegut* (www.thedailyvonnegut.com), a website exploring the work and life of Kurt Vonnegut.

Devon Balwit

is a teacher / poet from Portland, OR. She has two chapbooks: *how the blessed travel* (Maverick Duck Press) and *Forms Most Marvelous* (forthcoming with dancing girl press). Her work has found many homes, some of which are: *The Inflectionist Review*, *The Cincinnati Review*, *The Stillwater Review*, *Sierra Nevada Review*, *Red Earth Review*, *Timberline Review*, and *Glass: A Journal of Poetry*.

Jane Banning

lives in northern Wisconsin and has had over thirty of her stories, poems, and flash fiction writings published in various journals, including the *Boston Literary Magazine*, the University of Iowa *Daily Palette*, and *Long Story Short*, among others. She was a finalist in the Glass Woman Prize and the Micro Award. Her novel, *Silo*, is looking for an agent and while it's out looking, Jane goes kayaking.

Paul Beckman

was one of the winners in the 2016 Best Small Fictions with his story *Healing Time*. His stories are widely published in print and online and in the following magazines amongst others: *Connecticut Review*, *Raleigh Review*, *Litro*, *Playboy*, and *Thrice Fiction*. Paul lives in Connecticut and earned his MFA from Bennington College. Find his published story website here at www.paulbeckmanstories.com, and find his blog at www.pincusb.com. Paul hosts the FBomb NY flash fiction reading series monthly at KGB in New York.

Rick Blum

has been chronicling life's vagaries for more than 25 years as a nightclub owner, high-tech manager, market research mogul, and old geezer. His poems and essays have appeared in *Humor Times*, *Boston Literary Magazine*, and *The Satirist*, among others. Currently, he is holed up in his office trying to pen the perfect bio, which he plans to share as soon as he stops laughing at the sheer futility of this effort.

R. Bremner

has been published in various journals such as *International Poetry Review*, *Pure Slush*, *Paterson Literary Review*, and *Quarterday*. His latest eBook is *Kerouac Dreams, Kerouac Visions*, available at fine eBook retailers everywhere. Ron has evolved through metrical, Beat, and Surrealism to his current obsession with Absurdism. Absurdism is the only poetry which makes any sense to him in an absurd world. Visit him at https://www.pw.org/content/r_bremner, where milk and cookies await.

Gordon Brown

grew up in the deserts of Syria and now lives in the deserts of Nevada. Since his arrival in the New World his work has appeared in *Danse Macabre*, *Zetetic: A Record of Unusual Inquiry*, *The Kaaterskill Basin Literary Journal*, and *The Fable Online*. Gordon spends his free time looking after his cats, of which he has none.

Irene Buckler

taught in Australian primary schools for three decades, during which time she wrote many educational programs, stories for children and poetry, which have appeared in publications for children in the United Kingdom and in Australia. A flash fiction finalist in 2017's Hysteria (UK) and Field of Words Writing Competitions (South Australia), Irene's flash fiction stories may be found in various magazines and anthologies, in print and online.

Steven Carr

is an internationally published short story writer and playwright. He lives in Richmond, Virginia where his fingers are super glued to his computer keyboard. He has had short stories published in *Double Feature*,

Tigershark Magazine, *The Wagon Magazine*, *CultureCult Magazine*, *Fictive Dream Bento Box*, *Ricky's Back Yard*, *Visitant Literary Journal*, *Communicators League*, *Jakob's Horror Box* and a number of anthologies, among a laundry list of others.

Embe Charpentier

has had two books, *Beloved Dead* and *Sparks* – the first a ghost story, the second a book for struggling readers in high school – published by Kellan. Her work has appeared in a wide variety of zines and journals in print and on the internet.

Martin Christmas

lives in South Australia; has an M.A. in Australian Cultural Studies; and is a performance poet, photographer and theatre director. He has been published in Australian print anthologies, including *Friendly Street Poets*, and *Pure Slush*, as well as on the net in *Bluepepper* and *INDaily*. He teaches presentation elements to young poets and runs community poetry workshops. His first poetry collection, *Immediate Reflections* was published in early 2017.

Joe Cottonwood

has, by day, worked as a carpenter, plumber, electrician for most of his life. Some jobs were pretty; some, shitwork. Nights, he writes. Same split. Find more of his work at joecottonwood.com.

Doug D'Elia

was born in Holyoke, Massachusetts. He is a graduate of the University of Central Florida, and served as a medic during the Vietnam War. He is the author of three books of poetry, one of short stories, and his plays have been performed in five states. He can be found on Facebook at Doug Delia, and his web page is dougdelia.com.

Ruth Z. Deming

has had her work published in *Creative Nonfiction*, *Haggard and Halloo* and *Mad Swirl*. She is part of a Saturday Writing Group, which encourages writers to present a work every week. She is founder / director of New Directions Support Group for people and families affected by mood disorders. View the group's website here, www.newdirectionssupport.org, and view Ruth's blog here: www.ruthzdeming.blogspot.com. She lives in Willow Grove, PA, a suburb of Philadelphia in the USA.

Kristina England

is a writer and photographer residing in Worcester, Massachusetts. Her fiction, non-fiction, poetry, and photography have appeared in several magazines, including *Apeiron Review*, *Five 2 One Magazine*, *Gargoyle*, and *Zoomoozophone Review*. Follow her at https://www.facebook.com/kristinadengland.

Tom Fegan

spent his youth and college years working in the family business Burger & Shake in downtown Fort Worth, Texas. He worked for several years in the steel industry after college and is contentedly divorced. He is employed in the security industry, which allows him the freedom to pursue a writing career.

Alison J. Fish

lives in the Lacanian gap, a space of anticipation, where signifiers of the imaginary are linked between an unsymbolised real and an anchor of language. Gazing awry, she looks forward to looking back. As a bilingual writer and teacher with a penchant for whippets and purple skies, she dreams of owning a rocking chair and smoking a pipe. She regularly contributes to *Visual Verse* at http://visualverse.org/writers/alison-j-fish/.

Flora Gaugg

is a writer based in Adelaide, Australia. She has received recognition for both fiction and playwriting. She is interested in stories about ordinary people, and claims to be remarkably ordinary herself.

Mark Govier

may have been a sergeant in the Time Marines, and could be in the first assault wave in the Great Battle of 5359. To him, it was just last month – or he may have neglected to send a bio. You must decide for yourself…

Matthew Harrison

lives in Hong Kong, and maybe because of that his writing has veered from non-fiction to literary and he is currently reliving a boyhood passion for science fiction. He has published numerous SF short stories and is building up to longer pieces as he learns more about the universe. Matthew is married with two children but no pets as there is no space in Hong Kong.

Ashley Morrow Hermsmeier

has an MFA in Creative Writing from Pacific University and is currently an English and writing instructor in San Diego. Her work has appeared in *Michigan Quarterly Review*, *Flash Fiction Magazine*, *Funny in Five Hundred* and *Cease, Cows*, among others. Her story *When the Bees Come Back*, won *Gemini Magazine's* 2015 Flash Fiction Contest and was later nominated for a Pushcart Prize.

Mark Hudson

is an artist, writer, and poet, who has always been known for his "inane" behavior. In school, he was the class clown and always did silly things to get attention. Now, as a grown-up in what has become a very serious world, Mark finds that his humor oftentimes helps people through the sad things in life. As a poet, writer and artist, he's had his share of the ups and downs, but in his opinion, the most inane thing a writer can do is simply not write. A true writer or artist can't stop writing or painting or whatever, so don't be inane and join in the modern-day literary revolution.

A J Huffman

has had poetry, fiction, haiku, and photography appear in hundreds of national and international journals, including *Labletter*, *The James Dickey Review*, and *Offerta Speciale*, in which her work appeared in both English and Italian translation.

Abya Iyengar

is an internationally published poet and author. Her story, *The High Stool*, was nominated for the *Story South Million Writers Award*. She was finalist *at Flash Mob 2013*. Her recent works have been shortlisted for *The DNA-Out of Print* short story prize, *Brilliant Flash Fiction Contest*, and *The Strands International Short Story Competition*. Her published books are *Yearnings*, *Flash Bites*, *Shrayan*, *Many Fish to Fry* and *The Gourd Seller and Other Stories*. Find her website here at www.abhaiyengar.com and find her blog here at www.encounterabha.blogspot.in.

Susan Doble Kaluza

has work published in *Lost River Review*, *Rattle*, *Kentucky Review*, *Eunoia Review* and others. A former newspaper columnist, she recently quit her day job to work on a second chapbook. She is a competitive runner and former biathlete and two time national women's master's summer biathlon champion. She lives in the mining town of Butte, Montana, USA, and is the owner of a gorgeous white horse named Star.

Philip Kobylarz

is a teacher and writer of fiction, poetry, book reviews, and essays. His creative non-fiction collection *All Roads Lead from Massilia* is forthcoming from Everytime Press of Adelaide, Australia and he has a collection forthcoming from Brooklyn's Lit Riot Press titled *A Miscellany of Diverse Things*.

Donna Krause

lives in the suburbs in Willow Grove, Pennsylvania. She has a BA in sociology from Gwynned Mercy College, and has experience as a mental health therapist. She has suffered bipolar disorder for many years, and writes straight from the heart, often about her experience with her mental illness. An active participant in a weekly writing group, Donna has also been published in *Twisted Sister* and *Transcendent Visions*.

John Lambremont, Sr.

is a poet and writer from Baton Rouge, Louisiana, U.S.A. His poems have been published internationally in many reviews and anthologies, including *Pacific Review*, *The Minetta Review*, *Clarion*, *Raleigh Review*, and *Sugar House Review*, and he has been nominated for The Pushcart Prize. John's third full-length poetry collection, *The Moment of Capture*, will be published in June 2017 by Lit Fest Press. John's other poetry volumes include *Dispelling The Indigo Dream* (Local Gems Poetry Press, 2013), and a chapbook, *What It Means To Be A Man (And Other Poems Of Life And Death)*, (Finishing Line Press, 2015).

Neil Laurenson

mostly writes poetry. His debut pamphlet *Exclamation Marx!* was published by Silhouette Press in April 2016. Neil used to dress up as Tony Blair and assumed that people would interpret this habit as a protest rather than a tribute. He has since become a parent and a councillor and has resisted the urge to wear a latex mask to make a point. His children are grateful for this. Find more of his work at https://neillaurenson.wordpress.com/.

Tracy Lee-Newman

was a recent recipient of the UK-based Writers' Workshop bursary for 'rising stars'. In between steeling herself to send her first novel to agents and writing her second, she stays sane by penning short stories and drinking copious amounts of tea. Her work has been published by *Slingink*, *Secret Attic*, and *Centum Press*. Tracy lives in the south-east of England. You can follow her on Twitter @writeatme.

Larry Lefkowitz

has had stories, poetry, and humor widely published in journals, anthologies, and online. His literary novel, *The Novel, Kunzman, the Novel!* is available as an e-book and in print from Lulu.com and other distributors. Writers and readers with a deep interest in literature will especially enjoy the novel. His humorous fantasy and science fiction collection, *Laughing into the Fourth Dimension*, is available in print from Amazon books.

JP Lundstrom

grew up and attended college in southern California. Her writing most often is set in that warm, often dangerous place known as Los Angeles during the mid-twentieth century. Current books are *Adventures of a Young Girl* and *The Fruit of the Poisonous Tree*. She strives for easy reading, not that intellectual stuff; she doesn't like to waste too much time in deep thinking.

Michael Marrotti

is an author from Pittsburgh with a chemical imbalance and lack of patience. His writing has propagated the small press like chlamydia in Beechview. He's been faithfully volunteering at the Light Of Life Rescue Mission for the past three years now, the man believes in action. His chapbook *F.D.A. Approved Poetry* is available on Amazon.

Denny E. Marshall

has had art, poetry, and fiction published. Recent credits for fiction include *Postcard Shorts* and *50-Word Stories*. See more at www.dennymarshall.com.

Michael Mau

has had short fiction appear in *Black Warrior Review*, *Portland Review*, *Fifth Wednesday*, *Mount Hope*, *Firewords Quarterly*, *Punchnel's*, *Ferocious Quarterly*, and other places. 'An Open Letter to America From a

Public School Teacher', originally published in *McSweeney's*, received national attention when it was picked up by several news outlets. He received his MFA from the Bluegrass Writers Studio at EKU. Find his website at www.michaelmau.org.

Stephenson Muret

lives and writes in southern California. His plays, stories, essays and poems have appeared in scores of publications, touching virtually all genres.

Piet Nieuwland

worked on conservation management strategies in New Zealand after training as a forester. His poems appear in many places including *Landfall, Brief, Catalyst, We Society* and *Plate in the Mirror* anthologies, *Mattoid, Poetry NZ*, and *The Blue Note Review*. He reviews poetry for *Landfall Online Review* and is currently working on a collaborative art project with prison inmates and Northland poly-technical institute students.

Carl 'Papa' Palmer

of Old Mill Road in Ridgeway, VA now lives in University Place, WA. He is retired military, retired FAA and now just plain retired without wristwatch, alarm clock or Facebook friend. Carl, president of The Tacoma Writers Club is a Pushcart Prize and Micro Award nominee. His work appears in *Freak Pure Slush Vol. 13*. His motto: Long Weekends Forever. (Google "Carl Papa Palmer" to read more stories of poetry and prose.)

LaVa Payne

resides in the Piney Woods of East Texas where she writes stories, explores old sawmill towns, and gardens.

Melisa Quigley

is a writer and poet who has a short story published in RMIT University's anthology *Frayed*, poetry in Poetica Christi's anthology *Memory Weaving*, as well as poetry and stories in several issues of *Pure Slush*. She came second in the 2015 City of Glen Eira My Brother Jack Awards for her short story, *The House on the Hill* and commended for her poem, *Ice Cream*.

Stephen V. Ramey

lives in beautiful New Castle, Pennsylvania. Social worker by day, caped Trump-baiter by night, he is hard at work on his follow up to *Glass Animals* (Pure Slush

Books), a collection of post-progressive flash fictions tentatively titled *We Dissolve*. Watch for details at www.stephenvramey.com and @svramey.

Eliza Redwood

is a recent graduate of Binghamton University, and her work has appeared in *The London Reader*, *States of the Union*, and *200 CCs*. Find her @ElizaRedwood on Twitter.

Joseph Robert

has had fiction appear in *Kaleidotrope*, *Farther Stars*, *Mad Swirl* and the *Flash Fiction Press*. His poetry has appeared in numerous magazines and in 2015 he was longlisted for the Melita Hume poetry prize. His work has been reviewed in *Locus Magazine*, *SFRevu* and *Sabotage Magazine*. He is married to writer and poet, Leilanie Stewart.

Alex Robertson

enjoyed his formative years in Adelaide and spent his early working life around (country) South Australia and the Northern Territory. He has been published in university student publications and more recently in print and online journals. Since his location to the Adelaide Plains he has been involved in writing groups and broadcasting organisations around the north-eastern suburbs of Adelaide and Gawler.

Ruth Sabath Rosenthal

is a New York City poet, well published in the U.S., and also internationally. In October 2006, her poem *on yet another birthday* was nominated for a Pushcart prize. Ruth has authored five books: *Facing Home* (a chapbook), and four full-length books: *Facing Home & beyond*; *little, but by no means small*; *Food: Nature vs Nurture*; and *Gone, but Not Easily Forgotten*. The books are available from Amazon.com. Check out Ruth's websites: http://newyorkcitypoet.com and http://poetrybyruthsabathrosenthal.com.

Dimple Shah

arrived in Hong Kong eight years ago and promptly decided to forego a lucrative career in Banking and Finance for the unquantifiable joys of writing. An avid consumer of words all her life, she has only recently officially assumed the mantle of producer of words and spinner of yarns.

Martin Shaw

is fifty-two years old and has been writing for around ten years. Born in Luton, Bedfordshire, he then grew up in the Lincolnshire fens before moving to Cleethorpes. After being published in many online magazines, he now has his printed word appearing in the traditional paper press. He writes in the mornings and late evenings, and loves his family.

David Sklar

has more than 100 published works, including fiction in *Nightmare* and *Strange Horizons*, poetry in *Ladybug* and *Stone Telling*, and humor in *Knights of The Dinner Table* and *McSweeney's*. David lives with his wife, their two barbarians, and a secondhand familiar in a cliffside cottage in northern New Jersey, where he almost supports his family as a freelance writer and editor.

Anamarija Slatinec

is an Australian writer living in Sydney. She spends most days reading, writing and making impassioned speeches about things nobody cares about. She has been referred to as "delightfully strange", which she liked, and her parents say her writing is wonderful, so it must be true. She is currently working on a novel so stay tuned. You can find her on Twitter @Ana_Slatinec and her blog anaventures.wordpress.com.

JJ Steinfeld

lives on Prince Edward Island, where he is patiently waiting for Godot's arrival and a phone call from Kafka. While waiting, he has published seventeen books, including *Would You Hide Me?* (Stories, Gaspereau Press), *Misshapenness* (Poetry, Ekstasis Editions), *Identity Dreams and Memory Sounds* (Poetry, Ekstasis Editions), *Madhouses in Heaven, Castles in Hell* (Stories, Ekstasis Editions), and *An Unauthorized Biography of Being* (110 Short Fictions Hovering Between the Absurd and the Existential, Ekstasis Editions).

Leilanie Stewart

is a writer and poet. Her fiction has appeared in *Scarlet Leaf Review*, *Weirdyear*, *Linguistic Erosion*, *Pound of Flash*, *Mad Swirl*, *The Neglected Ratio*, *Ariadne's Thread*, *Absinthe Literary Review*, *Sarasvati*, *The Crazy Oik*, *Stanley the Whale*, *The Pygmy Giant*, *Wufniks*, *Carillon* and *Monomyth* and her flash story, *Twenty Questions*, was selected for the 'Best of the Web' Storm

Cycle Anthology 2014. Leilanie is also the Editor in Chief of Bindweed Magazine and is one half of a literary couple with her writer and poet husband, Joseph Robert. Her blog is at https://leilaniestewart.wordpress.com.

E. M. Stormo

is an editor by day, writer by night, and a teacher and promoter of musical literacy at all times. His recent fiction has appeared in *404 Words*, *The Conium Review*, *Entropy Magazine*, and elsewhere.

Jerry Vilhotti

has had two collections of works published. The first, *Gods Depicting Pastime*, has the Greek gods discovering a game once played by people – who plastered their bodies with empire blue to be one with the sky, and tried to figure out what the tic infested thing was all about. The second collection, *Specs in the Eyes of Seeing*, follows a little boy's long journey from childhood to manhood.

Rob Walker

rob walker *(n)*

pron./rob wȯkə /

1. a cantankerous curmudgeon with a titanium knee
2. an original cliché
3. www.robwalkerpoet.com

Michael Webb

is proud to be published in a number of *Pure Slush* titles while he sells drugs outside Philadelphia, Pennsylvania.

Allan J. Wills

tried to break the ice, when seducing the unknown Japanese woman who became his wife, by reading to her from a book of Australian jokes. Fortunately he realized that while laughter is universal across cultures, a joke is often balanced in the absurdities of just one culture. On their second meeting she responded to his effort with a gift of a CD of Rakugo performances.

Jeffrey Zable

is a teacher and conga drummer who plays Afro-Cuban Folkloric music for dance classes and Rumbas around the San Francisco Bay Area. His poetry, fiction, and non-fiction have appeared in hundreds of literary magazines and anthologies. His recent writing has appeared in *Serving House Journal*, *Chrome Baby*, *Mocking Heart Review*, *Kairos*, *Dead King*, *Ink In Thirds*, *Tigershark*, *Drunken Llama*, *Jokes Review*, *Third Wednesday*, *Fear of Monkeys*, *Futures Trading* and many others.

Also from Pure Slush Books

http://pureslush.webs.com/store.htm

Freak Pure Slush Vol. 13

978-1-925536-15-7 (paperback) / 978-1-925536-16-4 (eBook)

Summer Pure Slush Vol. 12

978-1-925536-13-3 (paperback) / 978-1-925536-14-0 (eBook)

Also from Pure Slush Books

http://pureslush.webs.com/store.htm

tall...ish Pure Slush Vol. 11

978-1-925101-80-5 (paperback) / 978-1-925101-98-0 (eBook)

Five Pure Slush Vol. 10

978-1-925101-71-3 (paperback) / 978-1-925101-72-0 (eBook)

Also from Pure Slush Books

http://pureslush.webs.com/store.htm

Feast! Pure Slush Vol. 9

978-1-925101-62-1 (paperback) / 978-1-925101-63-8 (eBook)

Rattle of Want by Gay Degani

978-1-925101-67-6 (paperback) / 978-1-925101-68-3 (eBook)

www.ingramcontent.com/pod-product-compliance
Lightning Source LLC
Chambersburg PA
CBHW031605260626
47154CB00020B/1587